About the Author

Vidya Math is a Cambridge-based author, who was born and brought up in Scotland. As a child, she loved books and dreamt of writing them. Her life's other works have included scientific discoveries in Microbiology, running a dance school and performing dance. She is also a songwriter, with a love of poetry. Vidya is currently working on a sequel to *The Book of Stamps*.

The Book of Stamps

Vidya Math

The Book of Stamps

Olympia Publishers
London

www.olympiapublishers.com
OLYMPIA PAPERBACK EDITION

A CIP catalogue record for this title is
available from the British Library.

ISBN: 978-1-80074-693-0

This is a work of fiction.
Names, characters, places and incidents originate from the writer's
imagination. Any resemblance to actual persons, living or dead, is
purely coincidental.

First Published in 2022

Olympia Publishers
Tallis House
2 Tallis Street
London
EC4Y 0AB
Printed in Great Britain

Dedication

For Su

Acknowledgements

Thank you to Su, the little girl who inspired the book, and to Mum and Dad, who took me to the library every week, so I could read all the books I wanted to. Thank you also to the authors who inspired me and to Ben for his enthusiasm for the book.

The Book of Stamps

The twin suns set on the horizon — Paolon and Safera, their benevolent golden outlines offering the final rays of warmth for the day. In the distance, the moon — Comera, risen already, shone its own reflection of the twins' power, ready and equipped to take over night duty.

Othelia, with pretty pink bows still in her hair, sat on her bed in a crisp, yet soft, nightgown, decorated in a delicate pattern of printed, purple diamonds on a background of innocent white. Poised on her crossed lap, lay The Book of Stamps, open at an embossed page, over which she ran the tips of her little fingers: the sensations of the pictures were almost as descriptive as the stories of the characters they immortalised.

The Old King — with his sallowed complexion, looking vaguely sad on the stamp that was orange.

The Shepherd — tending his flock on the pastures, was textured in brown.

The Dancing Girl — on the sparkling, iridescent, violet stamp, skirt swirling and face shining, as though she might come alive any moment.

Othelia smiled as the darkness fell. There was no time for a story tonight — the party had gone on too late and she could still hear the clattering dregs of her parents' guests attempting their exit. There was all the time to dream, though. She folded the book closed, laying it gently on the cushioned footstool by her bed, extinguished the night-light and slipped under the quilted comforter on her bed.

The open curtains framed the dusky light from Comera that flowed lazily into the room to envelop her. A cool breeze drifted in through the gaping window to blow a few kisses goodnight onto her cheek. Othelia drifted, with the breeze, into sleep, where a story from The Book of Stamps awaited her arrival.

The Old King

King Orion walked slowly through the corridors by the courts of his palace. His wearied step hinted that his son, the young prince, might see his own time of reign in a future not far off. The old king, today, escaped his well-meaning attendants, who guarded and guided him. He wished to walk the steps of his choice alone and on this rare occasion, the ruler of the land managed to get what he wanted.

He made his way to the main court, quietly thrilled that no flat-shoed footsteps had located him to run to his side and serve their duty.

The old queen was already sat in her throne, as the court rose to greet the king. She had gathered her velvet mantle around her — the scientists and engineers of the land were still some ways from inventing adequate means of indoor heating. The stone palace was as cold as the grey of its stones. Sometimes, it almost felt like a prison.

The old king raised his hand as a signal to the courtiers to resume their seating and the inevitable carers of the king scurried over with worried expressions to pick up his mantle as he walked to sit on his throne.

The old queen welcomed him with a loving smile in her eyes.

"My King," she addressed him, gently tilting her head forward in acknowledgement of his arrival — he, forever her prince and she, forever the smooth-skinned princess in his eyes. He turned to her briefly and smiled at her with an all-encompassing affection in his eyes. Their silvered locks had not decolourised the images they had of the sleek, brown-black, shimmering hair they had once shared. The old king's beard even now could not hide his chiselled jawline from the old queen's youthful memory.

Court was in progress and the people of the land of Zohor brought their problems to burden their beloved king — he, whose strength could carry them all; he, whose wisdom knew no bounds. For decades he had ruled kindly, aided by the interiors of a private room in the palace: a room filled with tools of a metaphysical nature. In its portals lay the strength that supported his. For the good of all.

The Hunters

Othelia wandered towards the secret garden that was hidden through deep-green bushes, thick with foliage that sectioned off part of the grounds surrounding the house.

There were bows in her hair again and in the morning, she had been scrubbed clean, in scummy soap water, quite against her will. This had put her in a bad mood and there had followed much protest to the pretty, frilly frocks she had been presented with after. She had settled, instead, for her favourite cotton pinafore and a checked ribbon for her hair, to match. She had made up her mind to see Harry that day — as compensation for the affront of bathing that had so startled her temperament earlier.

After a picnic meal with her family and many aunts and uncles and their families, she stole away, having eaten very little, with a raspberry juice stain around her mouth.

She was not sure if anyone else actually knew of the secret garden: it was almost as if it appeared and disappeared sometimes when she scrambled through its leafy entrance. Some days, she could not find it, but today, she was determined to search for it until it was there.

As it turned out, she barely had to look at all, as she stumbled into it straight away, setting foot through its gate of bushes.

The light was dim inside, as always — a canopy of tree

branches and creepers intertwined guarded the garden as much from the skies as it was hidden from the ground around it.

She looked about, climbing over some stone relics, which spoke of constructions that were no more.

Each time she entered the garden, it seemed, she came in through a different point: not something that concerned her young mind, but a curiosity nevertheless.

This time, there grew small, red berries on bushes in the garden, their leaves so dark a green that it made the light seem even dimmer.

She stepped gingerly over twigs and plants that made coils and traps for her feet, venturing deeper into the garden. She stopped and stood for a while in a spotlight of sunshine that had broken through the covering above. As she stood, peering at the golden splash of sky overhead, she heard a sudden flurry of breaking twigs and by the time she looked back down, Harry was making his way to land beside her, with little grace or poise. He was in a bad mood, too.

"Othelia," he said, straightening his green, flower-cap as he perched on a nearby stone, frowning. "It's good you're here."

Othelia was glad. It was a good time for her to have come to the garden.

"Harry, I felt like coming to see you today," she smiled, pleased. "I brought you this." She unfolded a hand containing a gleaming ruby, not unlike a crystallized berry.

Harry's mood changed dramatically, as he became occupied with the jewel.

"Really, for me?" he asked, smiling now. "How very... precious." He gently encased it in his fingertips, flashed Othelia a smile and suddenly the jewel was gone.

"Thank you," he said, his eyes shining like jewels themselves. "Come," he said, taking her hand, the suit of green leaves that clung to his body visible now that he was standing — a little taller than Othelia.

"Where?" she asked, cocking her head to squint at him through the sunshine.

Harry inhaled with a new-found exhilaration, filling him like a robin-redbreast plumped up. His eyes glazed over, as they rose to look above Othelia to the thought of another place.

"We shall go to where the Hunters went," he explained, lowering his eyes to sparkle at Othelia briefly before he turned to begin their flight.

They travelled effortlessly and at speed over the broken twigs and foot-traps, which now posed no hindrance. It always seemed as such when Harry was around.

They ran for some time — Othelia had not a moment to catch her breath.

"Othelia, we must run!" Harry called out at one point, fuelled by the excitement of his vision. "We must run to see the things that are worth seeing!"

And shortly after, they came to a standstill, although Othelia was quite unsure as to when that had happened exactly. It was as though one moment they were running and then they were standing as though they had not run at all. There was time to catch her breath now, but she found no need to.

They stood on a large rock, which gave a pleasing view over a wide spring of clear water, trickling over smaller rocks and greenery that favoured a watery bed to a dry one.

There was no canopy cover here and although it was daylight, there was no sunshine to speak of, as such.

Harry loosened his hand from Othelia's little hand and

used it, olive-skinned and grubby from the earth, to gesture to the land he had brought her to.

"This, Othelia," he said with much ceremony in his voice, "is where the Hunters played." He turned to fix his gaze on her almost alarmingly, adding, "Their cruel games."

Othelia felt frightened for a moment, until Harry broke the atmosphere with a smile, flashing glinting teeth across his triangular jawline.

"They are gone now — they have been for many years," he explained, poking her cheek lightly, with his third finger, to ease her worry.

Othelia breathed a subconscious breath of relaxation, smiled innocently and asked, "Who are the Hunters, Harry?"

It did not occur to her to ask how he knew of them. Harry's accounts never gave the air that they needed questioning.

"We will eat some pochals while I tell you," he said, smiling still and climbing down the rocks, now.

Othelia followed, placing her feet in her small, cream sandals carefully into the crevices between the rock-plant foot-puzzle that formed the descent. She suddenly had a thought to look behind to see how the forest of the secret garden had opened onto the rock, but by then she was half-way down to the ground and saw nothing but rocks and twisted plants above her. Besides, she needed all her concentration to avoid slipping or losing her footing anyhow.

"What are pochals, Harry?" she asked as he helped her down the last few rocks.

He brought a hand round from behind his back; in it, he held a deep red fruit that looked like a giant berry.

"A pochal?" Othelia asked excitedly, as it looked inviting, unlike the fruit she avoided when her mother tried to make her eat something citrus that was too tangy, or a banana that made her feel sick.

She clasped it into her hands as Harry offered it to her and they turned a corner round the base of the rock to see three trees there, bearing a ripe abundance of the fruits.

Harry climbed the trunk of one until he could reach a branch, pulled off a pochal and landed back on the ground, biting into it with relish, looking at Othelia with the suggestion for her to follow.

Othelia sunk her small mouth into the fruit and fell to sit on the ground with the deliciousness and happiness that ensued on tasting the sweet, deep berry flavour.

Harry fell, too and they laughed and laughed, pausing to bite more of the fruit, before looking at each other and again bursting into fits of mirth that sent them sprawling.

Once the fruit was eaten, Harry sat up, berry juice staining half his olive-skinned face and most of the surface of each hand. He took on a most serious demeanour.

Othelia sat up too, obediently, aware that the story was about to begin.

"A long time ago," Harry began, in the manner of someone much older, "in the time of King Orion and his benevolent kingdom, there lived the sons of courtiers on the palace grounds; their fathers were friends to the king and so they were treated well, with nothing to want for and all comforts to their needs.

"These young men grew strong — their raven-black hair would shine with the healthy oils of their nutrition and their muscles were well developed from their sport of spear-throwing on the palace grounds."

"What did they throw spears at?" Othelia asked almost in

a whisper, lest the ghosts of the black-haired men should hear her.

"At wooden targets," Harry relayed knowledgably. "At first they would throw them at round circles of wood, painted in bright colours, each colour representing a different merit."

Othelia did not always understand the things Harry said, but she listened intently, whether she understood or not. She knew there was always something in his words that was worth hearing.

"But then," he continued, "as they grew to be men, their wooden targets changed to sculptures of animals: giant rabbits, peacocks, bears."

"Who made them?" Othelia asked.

"The old king's sculptor made them — fine sculptures and it pained him to know of what happened to his works," Harry replied. "The old king was wise, but not to the ways of all under his rule. The sculptor was sworn to secrecy and the crucifixion of his wooden animals took place in the woods that were hidden."

"Oh," said Othelia.

"But then the savage men's appetites grew — as is often the case with those whose bellies are always full," Harry carried on relentlessly. "They were thirsty for blood and soon their sights turned to more elusive targets — the animals of Elvador."

"Elvador?" Othelia looked up at Harry.

"This…" Harry said, spreading his hands across the horizon, "…is Elvador." His eyes were glinting once again.

"There are no animals here," Othelia said, looking around. "No rabbits, no bears," she confirmed, with a shrug of her shoulders, shaking her head.

"None now!" Harry sprang to his feet, then leant down towards her to ask in a husky tone, "Would you stay in a place where you feared for your life?"

Othelia looked scared again and Harry thrust a hand towards her.

"Come!" he said.

Othelia grabbed his hand and scrambled to her feet, wiping her other, gritty hand, covered in berry-stain, on her checked pinafore.

Harry took slow steps forward, glancing at her by his side, until the earth under their feet changed to a softer one and hollowed openings appeared in the side of the rock face.

"Caves," Othelia said, remembering a picture from a storybook her mother had once read to her.

"Where bears lived," said Harry. He turned, grabbing her other hand and they ran back towards the spring.

"Fish lived here," Harry painted a picture in the little girl's mind, "travelling from warmth to warmth. Rabbits ran by the water, hiding in holes that were hidden themselves."

Othelia's eyes were wide with wonder now.

"And they all went away," she said, feeling resigned, for she would have liked to have seen the fish shimmering in the spring.

Harry perched by the spring, cupped the water in his hands and splashed it over his olive-tinted face, shaking it off in reaction to how cold it was. He looked up at Othelia. It was getting dimmer now and his skin looked a bit grey under the dripping water.

"The old king never knew. His eyes saw only good, so the Hunters were revered still for their skills — the stealth with which they rode horses for races; the pinpoint accuracy with which they shot spears through the branches of orange trees to bring fruit to the ground… We must go," Harry concluded his account.

He rose, his face dried somewhat by now, to take Othelia's hand and then they were running again, up the rock climb, through the forest and suddenly they were back in the garden, below the hole in the canopy, although there was no spot of sunlight through it now — just a darkening blue sky.

Harry kept a hold of Othelia's hand until they reached the bushes at the edge of the garden. He pushed his hand through the thick, leafy growth and lifted some of it to show an opening.

"Thank you for the ruby," he said, smiling at her.

Then he was gone and Othelia stood on the other side of the bushes, the opening in them sealed.

It was colder now than when she had arrived for her adventure and she suddenly felt afraid and wanted her mother. She ran back towards the house with her head down and on the way encountered the soft folds of a skirt coming as swiftly towards her. Smooth, delicate arms scooped her into a cuddle against her mother's welcome warmth and she was flooded with the instinct to sleep.

"Othelia, my darling, where have you been?" her worried mother's voice cooed into her ear. "I've been looking for you, my love."

Othelia was hurried back up to the house in her mother's arms, after which her mother was breathless. She set Othelia down to stand on the floor, grabbed a cloth, dampened it and began to wipe the berry-stained face in front of her.

"Sorry, Mummy," Othelia offered, looking up at her mother.

"You make such a fuss about drinking things," her mother commented, as she rushed about her task. "You only like raspberry juice and when you drink that, the whole world knows about it. It's all over your hands, too! How did you manage that?" The question was more one for herself, partly in awe of the things she found her daughter capable of.

Othelia could not have answered the questions if she had tried. Her kind and attentive mother was busied with looking after her and there was no time amongst the fussing to explain about the day.

"My darling, your father wishes to talk to me about some plans he's making. Will you be a lovely and brush your teeth and go up to your room? I'll come and give you a goodnight kiss later."

Once in her room, clad in her cotton nightie, Othelia picked up The Book of Stamps. One of the stamps, she had not noticed before: embossed in black was the fine, chiselled face of a young man with shiny hair wielding a spear. Her parents were yet to read her the story of this stamp. When her father had first brought her the book, excited at his present to her in anticipation of the light in her eyes, he had read her a list of the stories she would be treated to: The Old King, The Dancing Girl, The Young Prince, The Shepherd, The Companions of the Prince… but there had been no such word as "Hunters" used.

She was glad to have not noticed the shiny, black stamp before and put the book aside more quickly than usual before climbing into bed.

As the day drew to a close and Othelia was sleeping soundly, her parents too, after much talk, retired slowly to their bedroom.

Othelia's father loosened his collar a little too wearily for a man of his age and Othelia's mother went to the mirror to remove decorations from her delicate features.

"Oh!" she said, in surprise at an empty concave in her earring. "I seem to have lost a ruby! I wonder where that went?" She rolled the earring between her fingers, wondering for a moment if she could think where the missing jewel could be.

In the secret garden where it was dark now, Harry perched, almost motionless and inanimate, staring into the distance. A passing breeze with a chill made him shiver. Between his fingers that were still covered in the juice of a pochal, he rolled a ruby...

The Young Prince

The next morning, there came a visitor to the abode of Othelia and her parents. Swathed in a shawl of deep folds and intense colours, her skirt swept the floor as she glided on sandalled feet through the kitchen entrance. Her black, wavy hair was matched by the rims of her eyes which were blackened with kohl. Set in the rims were large, piercing eyes, whose energy frightened Othelia a little.

"I shall work in here," the stranger-lady said, seating herself in a dining chair by the table, skirt spreading across the floor, as she spread bejewelled wrists in bell-sleeves across the edge of the table. She shot a smile with a raised eyebrow at Othelia and the little girl came round from behind her father's leg, where she had been hiding, to look at the lady; the big eyes of magic had immediately worked their mystery on the small spectator.

Othelia's parents had been scurrying about all morning. Of course, they had forgotten to mention what occasion had excited them so to Othelia, but she had nevertheless been caught by the bustle and infectious spirit that played in the air. Othelia herself had chosen a black ribbon for her hair and had insisted on wearing her mother's black-gem bracelet — much too big for her and ideal for making her feel a part of the important atmosphere that filled the house.

Othelia's mother, unsure of what to prepare for their

visitor, had wasted two sets of cakes, burnt in the heat of nervousness, while the twin suns blasted their light through the open door.

"Oh, oh," Othelia's mother had said in dismay on taking the second set of cakes out of the oven.

"My darling," Othelia's father had soothed his wife. "It doesn't matter."

Some biscuits had been spilled from a tin onto a plate, instead, to substitute the failed cake attempts; a large pot of tea was also made and set upon the table to be served in china cups with saucers. Othelia's father straightened chairs that did not need straightening; Othelia's mother brushed down her daughter's already clean pinafore and a concoction of other things that did not need doing were done in attempt to bring normality at a time when an unseen force unsettled the household so.

The energies eventually settled with the entrance of the lady who had been so actively anticipated — she, the picture of calm.

As the lady sat at the table, Othelia's mother offered her tea in a rattling cup. The lady asked instead for herbal tea (of which there was none) and declined the biscuits, on account of being allergic to them.

Othelia's parents sat down on chairs at either side of the table, feeling defeated.

Othelia stood, smiling now at the lady, twisting her mother's bracelet around her wrist in delight at having accessorised in a manner akin to the mysterious woman who had such an effect on her parents.

"We are making plans," Othelia's father said to the lady. "We were hoping you could guide us."

The lady smiled serenely, knowingly, looking at the table, tracing the lines in the wood with a long fingernail, before looking up sharply. She reached under the folds of her shawl to her side and brought out a velvet pouch, which she emptied onto the table. A medley of crystal gems of many sizes, cuts and hues tumbled out.

Othelia's mother and father looked at one another and Othelia drew closer to put her hands on the edge of the table and look at the crystals.

"Another gem," the lady said, smiling and raising her eyebrow at Othelia again. Othelia smiled back contentedly with the expression of a cabbage-patch kid and settled her chin on her hands.

The lady spread the crystals with her palm and asked Othelia's parents to pick their selection of stones from the abundance of choices. As they chose the crystals, one by one, the lady read each tinted rock by clasping it in a palm closed over with long fingernails, sometimes opening her hand to look silently into the stone lying there, glistening brightly in the light from Paolon and Safera. From each stone, she told a jigsaw piece of the story of the household. Othelia's parents joined hands across the table at one point, absorbed in listening to the wisdom of the woman before them. Othelia was charmed by the manner of the wise lady and soon laid her own fingers, fingernails on display, across the black gems on her wrist.

The lady spoke of people Othelia had not heard of, but whose mention and descriptions brought gasps from her parents with sudden tears appearing in their eyes.

Othelia, lost in the charms of the lady, heard little of what was said, but noticed at the end, that the lady sat, arms stretched across the table, holding a hand from each of Othelia's parents in each of her own palms; tears rolled down her parents' faces and they smiled through the tears in gratitude.

Later that day, after the departure of the lady, a contemplative calm had descended upon the household and Othelia's parents unpacked a few boxes they had begun to pack a few days earlier. The creases that had deepened on Othelia's father's face in recent weeks had relaxed and he sat that evening, in a chair he had pulled to the porch from the living room, with Othelia bundled on his lap, cradled against his arm, as he read to her the next story from The Book of Stamps.

In her hand, Othelia held a stone left by the wise lady earlier. The lady had raised her eyebrow at Othelia one last time as she had gathered her crystals, pushing a clear one towards Othelia discreetly. Othelia's parents had not noticed, as they had wiped their eyes and Othelia had gladly wrapped her hand around the rock, feeling a tingle in her spine from the moment she touched it.

She lay clasping the gem in her hand that evening while her father began the story of the young prince.

***

The wait for the young prince had been a long one. Peppered with joy and underlined with happiness as the king and queen's lives had been, the lines in their skin could be read as the remnants of worry, mingled with the sacrifices they had made for their land, Zohor. Their young lives, as king and queen (chosen by the merit of the king's blood and cursed by the responsibility of their position) had for many a year seen them devoid of the welcome distraction of a child's presence. They had counselled their subjects on the development of the land's children and spent much effort in creating the kind of environment for all others' children as they would have wished for their own. Many a small hand was held and helped by royalty in the path to growing up, but none of the small hands had been royal themselves. Until one day, years after the hope of her own child had sedimented in the queen as a feeling of sadness and lost desire, the happy tidings arrived of an imminent addition to the royal line.

The land rejoiced and soon an heir to the throne, the young prince, was born. A miracle to his parents — a seed, whose germination was, by then, unexpected to all, apart from the mysterious Wisdom hidden in the king's secret room of magical knowledge. The invisible Wisdom, whose voice could be heard through senses alien to the people of the land, communicated through materials such as crystal, that bridged a gap from the invisible to the visible.

The elusive Wisdom sang a song of welcome for the son of King Orion and Queen Nelatron: the vibrations of its song were heard as excitement on the morning of Prince Thallon's birth. A magic pervaded the land, bringing rosy cheeks to busied mothers who prepared arrangements of flowers to decorate the streets with, hung from trees that grew on the paving. Children, brought to the first presentation of the prince on the balcony of the palace, bubbled with laughter which reached up to the baby prince, tickling him to break a smile in his olive complexion. His little head was cropped with a shock of black hair — an amalgamation of the strongest shades of colours that grew on the heads of the king and queen.

As a toddler, the prince played with the sons of courtiers, caught in their games of childhood, with contests promoting a survival of the fittest.

At three years of age, the young prince followed his father into a room hidden behind a door through which no one else passed. How this happened remained a mystery, for neither his father, the king, noticed his small companion following his lead, nor could the queen or multitude of caring nannies catch the little boy as he ran from them that particular day. The fastest of the nannies turned a corner to see the prince disappear through the door and she stopped short, knowing that even very small princes were called to duty at the appointed time.

There, in the room, the prince was confronted with sights his young eyes had not seen before. On a table covered in purple silk, lay metal casts of geometric symbols and a large circle formed of crystal gems. A fan of white feathers lay on the table, too. High above in the ceiling, a skylight shone light from the twin suns onto the crystals and a myriad of glass bottles, which sat on a sill nearby. A burner sat by the bottles, wafting essences of the secrets of nature through the room and up to escape through open chinks in the skylight.

"Papa!" the prince called, to the king's surprise.

The king turned to see the small, wide-eyed child and laughed heartily, the sunlight catching sparks of grey visible in his beard of late.

"Have you come to learn of mysteries, young man?" he asked his son, amused. He picked the prince up, setting him on the table, by the artefacts already sat there.

The young prince laid his hand on a metal-cast star that was beside him.

"Oh," the prince said in surprise, feeling a vibration from the star that tingled the bones in his little hand.

"Ah, my Prince," the king said, lifting his son's hand delicately from the star. "This is much too strong for you, just yet. Let me find you something more gentle." He picked the prince up again and sat him in his arm to hold him over the circle of gemstones of many colours beaming rainbows of light.

In the centre lay a cluster of clear crystals, buzzing with inexplicable rainbows of their own. The king chose a small, rounded one of these and showed it to the little prince. The prince pursed his lips and surveyed the crystal with some interest, reaching out for it with his fingers. The king held it to the prince's cheek and the little boy giggled, feeling a tingle tickle his cheek.

The king, pleased to hear his son happy, carried the boy to a nearby table, upon which further curiosities rested. He selected a chain, made of tightly spun cloth, to which was attached an empty pendant holder made of silver spiral. The king secured the young prince's crystal into the spiral such that the metal spun all around it, clipped it shut and locked it, before gently placing the chain about the boy's neck.

"And so, my Prince, you start your learning early," he chuckled.

From then on, the prince would accompany his father on occasion to visit the room of mystery.

As he grew, he learnt that the answers to many questions and dilemmas lay in a wisdom that was unseen and elusive. He watched his father spin pendula over maps to choose the destinations of royal expeditions; he watched as his father set a heart-shaped rose quartz beside the scarf of a young subject, holding a clear quartz wand in one hand, asking for guidance on the best suitor for the owner of the scarf. On finding his answer, the king would turn to the prince and smile and the small boy would smile back, father and son sharing the serenity brought by divine knowledge.

One time, the young prince fell sick from eating bread that played with his digestion; he insisted on accompanying his father to the magic room, nevertheless. Once inside, his father set him by a plant and surrounded him with crystals of green hues until the boy looked lit up.

"Ah, my son," the king sighed, "you suffer the symptoms of all those who are sensitive to the etheric energies. The denser foods of Zohor do not suit you and never will." He stopped to look at his son and felt a tear bleed from his heart. "I shall teach you as best I can and wish for you that it is comfort that helps you marry matter with ether and not discomfort that drives you from your office."

The little prince was much too young to understand the wishes of his father, but enjoyed basking in the healing effects of the crystals and plant about him. He soon felt well enough to skip around the stone floor circling the magic table of visions.

Thus, the young prince grew to be a delicate man of delicate diet, versed in magic and alien to the boisterous games of his companions, the sons of courtiers, who grew strong in their bodies through energetic pastimes. But they would sit together for their schooling and the companions of the prince knew their places and were to him the brothers he did not have. He cared not for the rough talk they branched into at times, but a glance from him would convey to them that he sought a different music to his ears.

The boys were grouped with the daughters of courtiers when artistic pursuits of painting and pottery formed the syllabus. The presence of the girls brought a welcome complement to the temperaments of the boys and vice versa.

The young prince blossomed, loved by all, shining his light wherever he went. On his eighteenth birthday, the old king and queen presented their son with a velvet suit of green, with a cap to match, aware that he was about to begin his travels across the land of Zohor. A green stamp of the prince was entered into circulation to acquaint him to the subjects of Zohor. The cosmic forces had been kind to the king and queen, blessing them with the gift of young Prince Thallon. They prepared now to share him with the people and trees and animals that he would one day hold responsibility for.

The Dancing Girl

Othelia's day had been lit with fun. Her parents had taken her to join their friends and children at a fair in town. There had been toffees (of which Othelia had eaten too many), new ribbons to buy and other little fingers to link hands with and run to where there were no grown-ups and just much giggling instead.

In their escapist travels, the children came across some festive-looking folk, with coloured scarves tied to their wrists, swirling around, twirling perfect frames of supple bodies, leaping to music from strummed strings and beaten boxes.

The vibrant merry-makers had eye-catching expressions, big smiles and shone a feeling of flying on clouds to anyone they glanced at.

Their costumes, equally inviting, revealed secret colours and layers of softness as they danced about. The children danced with them in excitement, weaving among the silken folds and precisely placed feet in welcome, as the dancers laughed, encouraging their new, young recruits.

When the dance was over, there came a hearty applause from an appreciative audience, to celebrate the accomplished dancers. The dancers, pleased at having delighted the crowd, curtseyed and took embellished bows. The children, too, were applauded by their parents, who had found them and delighted in watching their unexpected display.

Othelia's mother scooped her child into her arms and twirled a while longer after the performance was over, until Othelia protested, aware that her playmates were assembling in a new venture.

Her mother released her and caught hold of her husband's hand instead. She made a comment over her shoulder that caused peals of laughter from her friends around — the friends with whom she had once upon a time stolen to where no grown-ups were...

That night, there was time for a bedtime story. Othelia's mother — dressed in pink and heart abloom from the day of joy in the outdoors — bundled her daughter into bed and opened The Book of Stamps.

"The dancing girl," she began, eyes sparkling...

***

One of the duties assigned to Prince Thallon was that of roaming the more remote parts of Zohor to ascertain the wellbeing of those who lived there — the trees, the animals and the people of the area.

On his travels, as ever, the young prince was received with joy by the inhabitants of any particular place.

"My boy," an old man almost blinded with age would say, patting the back of the young man, "I remember the grandeur of your birth; we celebrated you."

The old women would set him down sweetened, milk-like, oat drink with motherly affection, to build him strong. The prince remained delicate, though — elven and strong, instead, with an inner wisdom.

The plants and trees, which loved him so, would billow in

35

the breeze, showering him with flower petals. The prince would laugh and this delighted his woody friends; they were the green beings and green was his colour, too. Often, amongst leaves, the prince seemed to disappear entirely.

The animals of the forest would come to him with their enquiring eyes and dropping to his knee, the prince would converse silently with them to hear of their needs. The rabbits — ever buoyant and playful — had little care and needed only to enjoy his presence and commune with his energy.

The deer, so like the prince in their regality, would stand quietly as he placed his hand on their backs and he and the deer would collectively ponder the truth about their positions.

The small, marsupial bears would come to him with worried expressions, concerned for their young and disturbed by the harshness of less benevolent animals. The prince would look into their eyes with love and draw them into his arms, for theirs was ever a protective energy and they needed protecting, too.

On one such mission of service, the young prince was accompanied by the stamp artist. One of the favourite methods of distributing knowledge of the intricacies of Zohor around the land was to commemorate it in the embossed stamps that were sealed onto letters for posting. The stamps were treasured as the most accessible form of art in the land and from them, the peoples of Zohor learnt how to recognise their prince, their king, Queen Nelatron and also their brother and sister subjects who they never came into contact with.

The people of the City of the Palace learnt about the tending of sheep by a shepherd on the hills of Elvador — pressed for all to see, into embossed brown, shimmering paper: a portrait of information, so that the appreciation of the masses could travel through the air and uplift the shepherd on his lone mission to supply Zohor with wool for the winters.

The shepherd, in turn, learnt of the blacksmith, who smiled in exuberant happiness out from his grey stamp, one arm poised to pound heated metal.

Even the postman once sported a likeness of himself on the letters he carried, but no one was a stranger to the purpose of the postman. His stamp was but a celebration of the messenger. Several stamps of postmen had been made — all dressed the same, but with a variety of smiling faces to choose from.

And so it was, that on the eve of his nineteenth birthday, the young prince arrived at Melthon, a village set amongst the woods, to which a postman travelled weekly on a horse.

The daylight dipping by then, saw the prince, his artist companion and two sons of palace courtiers, dismount their steeds at a clearing fifty measures south of the City of the Palace. In the distance, a group of people buzzed, visible as animated wisps of different colours.

Thirsty from their journey, the prince and his fellow travellers led their horses towards the party of colours, anticipating a rest, accompanied by a soothing hydration from the characteristic drink of the region.

"This place is Melthon." The young prince smiled to the artist and sons of courtiers, acknowledging arrival at their destination.

"Perhaps there are beautiful women here," Romonon, one of the sons of courtiers said, a tinge of harshness in his voice complemented by the unnecessary severance of a blossom from its tree by a swift move of his knife.

The young prince shot Romonon a glance of fire and

breathed in deeply, shutting his eyes and steeling himself, as he heard the other son of a courtier, Palthon, laughing in support of Romonon's comment.

As the pink blossom thudded softly onto the leaf-carpeted ground, the artist, Palay, swooped to scoop it into his hand and lifted it to his nose. He looked at the prince offering a smile, and with it, composure for the prince's nerves, which had been tackled so by the sons of courtiers.

"My Prince," he said, holding the flower out to the boy who blended so well with nature's environment.

The prince accepted the flower and they walked to finish their journey, arriving at the colourful party they had seen from afar.

In the evening light, a gathering of children, faces shining and red from excitement, grinned as they patted footsteps onto the ground in random dance formations. Each looked healthily anointed by the dirt of the outdoors, with unkempt hair that spoke of the distance between the City of the Palace and Melthon. One or two children chewed on sweets that had been given to them by the jolly lute player, who sat poised on a tree stump, his own cheeks reddened from years of living a life of laughter, eating enjoyable food.

Embraced by the semi-circle formed by the children, a lone young lady danced, twirling under the stars that were beginning to show. Her skirt of purple, magenta, crimson and black, was set with tiny mirrors, off which glistens of light darted. A long ribbon, tied in a bow, dressed her hair and her wrist was decorated with droplets of gems that matched the iridescent colours of her skirt. She twirled until, mid-spin, her eye caught sight of the newly arrived visitors to Melthon.

The music from the lute slowed to a halt and the

movement of the children too stopped in curiosity of the newcomers.

The young prince tilted his green cap forward and removed it with a smile to the young lady and her party.

"Prince Thallon!" the lady gasped, bringing her fingers from mid-air to her lips in surprise. The delicate beauty of her face encased deep brown eyes that looked at him in wonder.

The prince raised his eyebrows — it seemed the stamp artist had painted a good likeness of the heir to the throne; he was recognised well across the land.

'Greetings, m'lady," the prince said. "And to your company," he addressed the lute player with a nod and the children with a wink.

The lute player rose from his make-shift chair, bowed to the prince and beamed some more.

"Come, sons," he said to the visitors, "you will be weary from your travels. We must feed you and give you a taste of the nectar of our fruits."

Romonon and Palthon looked the lady up and down with thoughts of their own. Palay extended a hand to the lute-player, Oberon and the young lady lined the children up, such that they might greet their prince.

The prince dropped to his knee as the children each told him their names, accompanied usually by a slice of information to tell of their day.

"It was harvest day today and we played in the grain," little Pottle told the prince.

The prince chuckled as he shook hands with each of the small subjects until there, at the end of the line, in the soft moonlight of Comera, stood the dancing girl, her rosy cheeks visible under a burning torch suspended nearby.

The prince rose to greet her.

"My name is Maria, my Prince." She introduced herself, bowing her head as he took her hand into his.

"Princess Maria, we call her!" Oberon called over his shoulder, as he turned to lead the amalgamated party a short distance into the heart of Melthon.

The next morning saw the prince and his companions rested from sleeping in a hay-loft — the most prized sleeping area in Melthon. The prince awoke to find a small cat curled asleep by his shoulder. He kissed it good morning in delight — as prince and privileged, his bed had forever been a lonely one, with no siblings or friends to share it in his palace bedroom.

A banquet was laid as breakfast by the people of Melthon, in celebration of the arrival of the heir to their throne.

Pitchers of raspberry juice were set on the breakfast table, as they had been on the supper table the night before, for raspberry juice was the speciality drink of Melthon, the village of berries.

At the end of the meal, Prince Thallon stood to address his hosts with a pleasing revelation.

"Good people," he said, raising a goblet in the air, "we have come in search of a new stamp — one to represent Melthon."

A cheer arose from the crowd for Palay, who stood to take a bow, as the prince gestured to him.

"And, my people," the prince continued, "I will know you today by learning of your lives — for your Prince has, for the first time, come to your village."

Through the crowd that encircled the royal breakfast table, the daughter of the alchemist, Maria, gently parted a pathway to walk towards the prince.

"My Prince, it is the day of your birth," she said, prompting another resounding cheer that lifted the prince on its joyous vibration.

"As a gift, we would like to share with you a secret," Maria said quietly, as though even speaking of it could rupture its casing and release it into the open.

A rumble of approval echoed through the crowd and the prince left his party to follow the princess of Melthon to a place where no village-outsider had hitherto been invited.

Palay, still applauding the gift chosen by the villagers, watched the prince leave with his light-footed guide, sure now of whom would be his muse for the next stamp he drew.

Romonon and Palthon broke their applause to swig two or three more mouthfuls of a variety of fermented, alcoholic juices, before passing each other looks that spoke of a common intention.

The prince watched the feet of Maria before him, guiding him over what was increasingly becoming tricky ground to walk on. The rocky surface changed to undisturbed woodland, into which Maria led the prince, turning to give him a smile of reassurance.

Suddenly, although the prince did not quite realise how or when, they entered a small, hidden clearing, unapparent outside its boundary, in which there stood three trees, bearing a few, large, berry-type fruits — the like of which the prince had not seen before.

"My Prince," the dancing girl turned to address him, "welcome to the Orchard of the Pochals."

"Orchard?" the prince asked, raising his eyebrows at her again in surprise.

The dancing girl laughed — the tinkle of her merriment delicious to the prince's ear; an involuntary spark of joy sprung to life in his heart. He stopped to look at her. Always, he was surrounded by the sons of courtiers — chosen for him by the tradition of palace ways. The young maids of the courts were busied with other duties, dictated by tradition and the prince had never happened to spend time in the company of a young girl alone.

"Prince Thallon, if ever you are sad, you should sit amongst trees, for they will love you till you feel better," she said.

Even as he stood listening to what she told him, the prince felt love infusing his aura.

"I know," he said gently, for he, too, had an understanding of the woods. "I shall heed your words."

The dancing girl smiled again, her cheeks round and as berry-red as the fruit in the branches of trees around her.

"You must dance for me, my Princess!" the prince proclaimed suddenly, a tinge of mischief lifting the corners of his mouth, influenced by the reassurance of the trees, the playfulness of unseen spirits of the wood and another energy which was new to him.

The dancing girl stopped smiling and raised the fingertips of one hand to her lips; oh, how he loved it when she did that.

"My Prince," she said with sudden composure, drawing her hands down to either side of her hips and tilting her head to look at him with a hint of reprimand, "you must not ask such things — for you are a prince and I, one day your subject to be. I must, thus, obey whatever it is you ask."

She frowned at him, in all seriousness.

"Then if it is so — you must obey," confirmed the prince,

thoroughly at one with the wood and its ways, now. He settled on the ground with his back to a tree, one leg outstretched and extracted, from an inner pocket of his jacket, a piccolo cut from bamboo.

For a moment, a look of disbelief crossed Maria's face, before she too became affected by the intoxicating energies that were abounding. She broke into a giggle and began to sway to the drifting notes of the prince's piccolo.

Before long, the dancing girl was twirling, enchanted by the atmosphere and encompassed by the prince's melody, looking as ethereal as though her alchemist father had conjured her from some magical transformation.

As the music drew to a close, Princess Maria stopped abruptly, skirt still swirling, and thrust her hand in the air in a grand gesture of finale. The force of the movement caused a gem to dislodge from the bracelet on her wrist and the small, round bead dropped to the ground amongst the leaves and plants that carpeted the earth in cushioned peace.

The dancing girl brought her fingertips to her lips again and the young prince leapt to his feet to search for the gem. Spying a glisten by her feet, he knelt to rescue the small ruby that nestled there. He wrapped his own fingertips around it and raised it on his palm to offer Maria, a look of apology shining through his imploring eyes.

Maria smiled at him, poked his cheek tenderly with her third finger a few times to alleviate his guilt at the consequences of making her dance and accepted his offering.

"My Prince," she said, walking over to one of the three, fruit-bearing trees in the orchard.

The prince rose to his feet and followed her, close behind.

She lifted her hand to touch one of the large, berry-like

43

curiosities.

"This is our secret — our gift," she said happily, easing the fruit off its branch into her palm. She held it out to the prince.

"It's a pochal. The only place you will find one is here," she told him.

The prince took the fruit from the dancing girl, as she nodded encouragingly for him to try it. He sank his teeth into its soft flesh, to be filled with a delicious sensation that made him laugh out loud.

Maria laughed also and took a bite out of the pochal as the prince held it out for her to eat, too.

They collapsed against the tree, filled with merriment, brought on by the juice of the pochal. The spirits of the wood laughed with them too.

"My Princess!" Prince Thallon exclaimed, amid gusts of laughter, catching Maria's hand and pressing it to his heart. "You must join me on my travels — we will journey to places far from all those that are known of. We will write new history!"

The pair collapsed to the ground then and writhed with laughter so deep, it was as though they had gone mad.

"Prince Thallon," Maria said, sitting up and sober now, recovered from the episode, "we may see pochals on one of our travels then."

The young prince, sobered too, looked at her inquisitively.

"The soil of Melthon, it is thought, is the only one that supports the growth of the pochal tree," Maria continued, gesturing to the three trees. "These trees are hundreds of years old, and it is said that it even takes hundreds of years, no less, for the seed of a pochal to bear fruit upon planting. We have tried to grow the seed of the pochal, but even Melthon is blessed with only these three trees that ever grew to bear this fruit of the divine."

"Then why is it you feel we may see the fruit yet elsewhere?" the prince asked, intrigued.

"Oh, not now," Maria clarified. "It will be many a year before that would be possible." Then, with a look of confession and a lowered tone in her voice, she said, "Prince Thallon..."

"Yes?"

"I have another secret. You remember the stamp of the shepherd?"

"I remember," the prince grinned, for the portrait had been his own choice and the result of a prior mission.

Maria blinked a couple of times before edging closer to the prince, whispering, "I sent him pochal seeds — one from a fruit of each of the trees."

She sat back as though, since the crime was over, it was time to forget about it.

"Is he a friend of yours?" the prince asked, surprised, as the pastures of Elvador, roamed by the shepherd, lay seventy-five measures west of Melthon and were rarely, if ever, visited by residents from the rest of Zohor.

"Not a friend," Maria shook her head. "I do not know him at all. But when I saw the land on his stamp, I thought perhaps he knows of a place where pochals would grow. I wrote a request for the planting of the seeds — I did not tell him what they were, for that would have been wrong."

The dancing girl looked quite uncomfortable now and the prince was amused at her sweet guilt. He reached over, prodded her cheek with his finger gently to make her smile and after a while, they set off through the portal in the bushy boundary of the orchard, back to the centre of Melthon, where the stamp artist was waiting ready with poised paints.

**

Othelia's mother closed The Book of Stamps. Othelia, asleep already, dreamt that night of pochals and thought that Harry would have liked the dancing girl very much.

Othelia's mother smoothed a stray lock of hair from her daughter's forehead to plant a kiss there.

"Sweet dreams, my darling," she whispered.

The Shepherd

The next morning saw an array of business associates of Othelia's father's arriving at the house. Othelia's mother had painstakingly set the table in the dining room with refreshments and had aired the room by throwing open all the windows it had.

Paolon and Safera shone through the open curtains benevolently, smiling their support.

Othelia's father, dressed in a smart shirt, and neat-cut trousers, carried bound papers from his study and placed them in the centre of the dining table.

Othelia followed her mother, who carried a satin tie, into the dining room. She watched her mother fix the tie round her father's collar and fuss over him to make sure he looked presentable. The little girl did not ask her parents what the fuss was about — they rarely remembered to brief her on matters of the grown-up world; instead, she waited patiently, watching rainbows forming in the sunlight on the cut-crystal exterior of a decanter.

Her father looked over to wink at her and her mother turned to usher her out of the room into the kitchen.

Lifted onto a high stool in the kitchen, Othelia sat swinging her legs.

"Othelia, my darling," her mother said, busily wrapping some sandwiches and pieces of fruit in brown paper, "I need you to play in the gardens today." She filled a small, glass bottle with a berry squash and pushed the bottle, along with the paper food parcel, into a colourful, cloth satchel.

Othelia did not need to be asked twice, as she had already intended to go and see Harry that day. She wanted to tell him of the dancing girl and the shepherd who roamed the pastures of Elvador.

The kitchen was situated at the side of the house, such that its door looked out onto a yard that led to a porch that housed the front door. Through the open door of the kitchen, Othelia saw several, middle-aged gentlemen, dressed like penguins, arriving at the front door of the house to form a queue. Her mother yelped at the sight of them, picked Othelia up off the stool and deposited her on the floor, hurriedly placing the satchel over a small shoulder and ran off through the house to open the front door.

Othelia stood by the open door of the kitchen, fingering the satchel, watching the businessmen light up with a "Hello!" as they disappeared, one by one, into the front door.

She looked round to see if the boiled sweet jar, full of what looked like marbles made of sugar, was still hiding by the side of the fruit bowl. Her mother and father usually only allowed access to it on special occasions. This was such an occasion — she was going to see Harry...

As she began her trek across the gardens to Harry's secret enclosure, the businessmen and her father settled into a meeting about the fields of the region, its flanking districts and other select areas.

"Whatever we decide," Othelia's father said to the men, shielding his eyes from the sunshine as he showed them to their seats, "we must work for the benefit of the people and of the land."

A rumble of agreement arose around the table and optimism was heightened still at the sight of the refreshments Othelia's mother had so carefully prepared.

One of the attendees, Gordon — a red-haired farmer, who had prospered through growing varieties of lavender that had become much sought after — nodded his head.

"Aye," he agreed. "We must care for the pastures as they care for us. We have nought without them."

Delek, another of the gentlemen added, "And the animals, too."

And so, the meeting progressed, under the inquisitive eyes of colourful birds that flew to the window to add their support.

Othelia, now approaching the secret garden, stopped for a moment and looked around to get her bearings. For some reason, things looked a little different today. Most of the bushes at the entrance to the garden were in bloom of some sort or another. One bush sported the most incredibly vibrant, orange-pink roses. She drew closer to touch their velvety petals, but no sooner had she raised her fingers to the flowers, she felt her foot stepping through a space and suddenly she stood on the other side of the bushes.

Unlike before, the secret garden today had no canopy of dark green and a plethora of flowers lit it up in an array of welcoming colours.

Harry, for once with a smile on his face, sat on a fallen tree amid the periphery of blossom and beamed at Othelia as she focused on him. Although still dressed in a medley of green leaves, Harry's attire seemed unusually lighter in shade and was even peppered with the odd flower petal providing splashes of colour here and there. His flower cap was positively white, with but a hint of green.

"Today is a good day," he said to his visitor.

"Hello, Harry," Othelia said, ambling over to sit on the tree trunk with him.

"You wanted to talk about the shepherd?" Harry asked, turning to look at her.

Othelia scrunched her face at him, puzzled as to how he knew.

"I am your friend," Harry explained. "Friends understand each other."

Othelia smiled and caught sight of something he held in his hands.

"What are you holding, Harry?" she asked him as he held up a bow made of two rose petals from the orange-pink blossomed bush she had been so taken by. The petals were bound in the middle by the long strand of a creeper, the two ends of which hung down like a makeshift ribbon.

"For you!" he said, as though almost surprised himself.

Othelia, delighted, clapped her hands.

"Mummy didn't have time to tie my hair up today!" she said, enthralled at the coincidence.

She turned for Harry to put it in her hair, which he made a mess of, but this bothered no one.

Othelia took her satchel off from about her shoulders and sat it between them, on the tree trunk. Harry's eyes twinkled as she extracted six marble-like sweets — each of a different colour — from the bag. She deposited them all into his cupped hands and sat back, pleased that her job was done.

Harry looked pleased too, rolled all the 'marbles' into one palm and (almost in danger of dropping them out of his small hand) sprung up from the tree trunk. He strode over to a peculiar bush, sporting bright blue flowers.

Othelia, ever influenced by her intriguing friend, jumped off the tree trunk to follow him.

As they stood by the blue-blossomed bush, Harry picked a blue 'marble' out of his palm and held it by a flower; they were the same colour.

"The essence of avelyn," he said, closing his fingers over the sweet and opening them to show it broken into two halves.

Giggling, Othelia pushed one half into Harry's mouth and another into her own. The sweet tasted of flower petals — blue flower petals and for a moment, Othelia thought that she had never seen any such blue sweets in the hidden sweet jar before.

Harry, giggling too now, skipped over to a neighbouring tree from which feathery lengths of crimson blossom hung. Again, he took a 'marble' from his diminishing supply and, as before, the colour of it matched the flowers he held it against, perfectly.

"Harry, you're silly," Othelia told him, giggling uncontrollably as she repeated her feeding duty when the sweet fell open into two halves. This sweet was rich with a crimson flavour that tantalised the back of their tongues and travelled to the base of their spines as a tingle. They both stood on their toes and closed their eyes tightly, in an attempt to withstand the strength of the feeling, until they gave up, roaring and screaming with laughter, as though they were monkeys swinging through trees.

And so, the ritual continued to reveal a lilac 'marble' against lilac roses, a green one against the grass, a golden one against Paolon and his twin Safera, and finally, an orange-pink one to match Othelia's bow. This was Othelia's favourite and tasted of peaches, giving her a glow in her tummy that tickled her heart.

The sweets lit up every part of their beings.

"They would make good colours for stamps," Harry noted aloud, with a sudden authority.

Othelia looked at him, attentively, before saying, "Harry, I think you would have really liked the D—"

"Are you hungry?" Harry interrupted, a sudden colour rushing to his face, making him look almost upset.

Othelia, too, was overcome with a wave of upset that twisted in her stomach. Her face began to pucker and tears rose to her eyes.

In response, Harry quickly grabbed both her hands and began to spin her round him with gathering speed until her feet could not keep up and she screamed for him to stop. By the time that happened, the emotion that had gripped them so a few moments before had been dissipated in the spinning and they settled to investigate the contents of Othelia's satchel.

Harry ate the pieces of fruit while Othelia munched on the sandwiches.

Harry, with a few splashes of fruit juice decorating his face, said, "The shepherd loved the colours of the land. His heart was always bursting with thoughts of the earth, its animals and the golden sky that gave rise to all of it. In the time of King Orion, Elvador was the village with the richest soil in all Zohor, fed by the fresh streams that pervaded through it."

Othelia soaked up the feel of Harry's words, not worrying about whether she understood them or not — the feeling they gave her was descriptive enough.

"In his home," Harry continued, "were a thousand tributes

to the flora and creatures he spent his days with. Oh, his sheep's wool kept him warm in winter, all right, but a multitude of other emblems kept his spirit warm, including colourful paintings of lotus flowers, shimmering, blue dragon-flies, the setting suns, Comera in her nightly cloak, the red of strawberries, the blue of avelyn..."

They sat quietly for a while, exploring the shepherd's home in their minds.

"It was the young prince's first quest for a stamp that brought him to the pastures of Elvador." Harry's account took on a more sober tone. "On his eighteenth birthday, a stamp had been made of him at the request of King Orion and with it, the responsibility of stamp-making presented to the prince as one of his first duties in training to become the leader of the land.

"He accepted the task with joy and not long after, set off on his first adventure to give portrait to a scene from Elvador. The stories the prince had heard of Elvador had planted a longing in his heart to visit the peaceful place. The seedling of longing had blossomed into a calling and blessed with his new office, the prince prepared for travel.

"The evening before the journey, after sweet briefings from his parents, the prince wandered into palace woodlands in the last light of the day. His heart trembled somewhat in the anticipation of the responsibility he had. He wished, as always, to bring light to all he encountered; such sweetness prevailed in his heart...

"He clasped the crystal gem his father had given him many years ago in one hand — still it hung in a pendant-holder from his neck, its chain longer now. In his other hand, he held a larger, clear-quartz, cut stone — one for Elvador.

"For decades, the kindly king had charged such stones

with benevolence from the palace, distributing them across Zohor, burying them in the soils of the villages, the moss-carpeted grounds of the moors and sinking them into the sands of beaches. This tradition, known previously only to King Orion and Queen Nelatron, had now passed in secret to their son. Blessings were contained in the crystal; a wish for strength and a link to the palace and all of Zohor lay in the ice-like clarity.

"Once, there had been a failing of crops in Capilla, the village of corn. Its ambassador rushed from the fair village, sixty measures on his horse, to the Palace of Orion to ask for help.

"The king had soothed the ambassador's worries and requested a night's stay of comfort at the palace for the distressed man.

"The king then retreated to the room of mystery for guidance on the plight of Capilla and other matters of the day.

"In the circle of crystals on the table in the room, the king placed a larger, clear quartz crystal and called upon a link to Capilla, where there lay buried a sister quartz to the large one on the table. He asked for knowledge about the corn crops and there appeared to him the vision of a type of jolly insect, increasing in number, feeding on the corn supplies.

"'Why do you eat the food of the people?' the king asked the souls of the unassuming insects.

"'We like the corn,' the insects replied. 'It makes our bellies round and then we feel nice.'

"'But gentle ones,' the king reasoned, 'it is not your business to eat so heartily: for you, as with all other creatures, are here for a mission; you are not here to gorge yourselves to the point where you malfunction.'

"The souls of the insects thought for a moment.

"'We did not mean to eat the food of the people,' they said. 'We were just playing.'

"The king listened patiently to these small subjects of his, amused at their sweet mindlessness, enjoying the vision of them, for he would not normally have seen them with such clarity.

"'Perhaps you could eat the corn as a special treat, on occasion?' the king suggested.

"The insects were pleased with this, for it mattered not to them whether they ate the corn or not — there were plenty of other things to eat; they had just happened upon it as a new pastime.

"The following day, Capilla's ambassador, rested but worried still, addressed the king once again, in court.

"The king, amused still, at the thought of his insect subjects feasting on Capilla's corn, advised the ambassador to inform Capilla's corn-growers to place an offering of the grain about their fields on special occasions and all would be well.

"Such was done and the corn-crops were restored happily. On each special occasion — harvest, New Year, eclipses — corn was offered on the fields by the corn farmers; it disappeared by the next morning and gentle, round-bellied insects rolled unseen, in mirth..."

Othelia giggled, listening to Harry's account, picturing the funny insects having their play.

"Harry, you're silly," she managed, through spurts of giggles.

"Not I!" Harry denied, springing up from the tree trunk. "'Twas the king. He taught his silliness to his son, the sweet prince." He sat down again to resume his story.

"And so it was that Prince Thallon strode through the forests of the palace grounds the night before his journey to Elvador, wishing to charge the appointed crystal with the benevolent energies of the area.

"He wandered too far, lost in excitement and distracted from reality, until he stumbled upon a figure, outlined in the night-light of Comera.

"He approached the static being to inspect it and for one moment, the light of the moon glinted off the surface of Elvador's crystal to illuminate the figure — a large, wooden rabbit, whose head had been speared through and split almost totally from its body."

Harry stopped his account and stared ahead, without blinking.

Othelia looked at him with eyes just as wide.

"Harry," she said, distressed.

He turned to look at her, his eyes like stone.

"The palace courtiers' sons, Palthon and Romonon — colleagues of the prince — had been appointed to journey with him on his travels," he said.

Othelia said nothing, looking at him still — she too was unblinking now.

Harry drew a breath, turned to look ahead of him again and continued. "The party of four — Thallon, Palay, Palthon and Romonon left for Elvador the next morning."

Harry slipped off the tree trunk to stand on the leafy ground in front of it.

The mood had dipped and the vibrance of the many colours of flowers around the two conversationalists had diminished somewhat.

There came, at that point, a chirruping bird, flying over

the bushes that guarded the secret garden from the other grounds of Othelia's father's house.

The bird, fresh from watching the goings-on in the dining room, had so endeared the businessmen farmers that they had fed it a biscuit crumb, as a celebration on deciding to abolish permission for hunting in the regions they were responsible for.

The bird, infused with their joy, flew over the grounds of the house and swooped into the secret garden, where Harry stood with his head hung and Othelia sat with a lump in her throat.

The cheery bird fluttered about them, joyful with life itself, making such a scene that she caught the attention of the small pair who felt so sad. She circled Othelia a few times before flying up to Harry's face, chattering incessantly until her enthusiasm infected the leaf-clad boy and his little friend with the bow in her hair.

Task completed, the chirpy bird flew off leaving a lightened Harry and Othelia to continue their mission of the day.

Harry told of the arrival of the stamp party to beautiful Elvador, where the shepherd, a peaceful, young man, tended a giant flock of sheep on the rocks of Elvador.

The animals — each with a name — communicated with the shepherd, pouring love into him. The shepherd, while tending his crowd, would paint pictures of his beloved Elvador, lush with plants blossomed in many colours, grown in the richest soil in Zohor.

"My Prince," he told the slender man dressed in green, as they sat upon a rock overlooking a stream, "my aim is to paint pictures of all the birds and animals who live here."

As if it had heard, a peacock danced in the distance, displaying an artist's treat of colours in its feathers.

The shepherd took the prince to a cave at the foot of the rock, outside which a family of bears meandered, the two bear cubs socking each other softly in twin jest.

The mother and father bears strode over to greet the shepherd and their prince, growling their words in bear language to express their warm delight at the prince's visit.

On the night of the painting of the stamp, after the shepherd had sat, appreciated, as he appreciated his countryside, the prince left the merrymaking at the shepherd's house to steal in secret to the stream. Once there, he buried the crystal for Elvador in the bed of the stream, before turning to go and spend a final night in the company of the shepherd and the few peoples of Elvador.

Behind him, four bears should have been sleeping peacefully in the cave. Instead, as the prince had removed the crystal from a pouch, where it had been hidden by his side, to bury it, a glint of Comera's moonshine had slid off the crystal to momentarily illuminate the scene of a mother, father and brother bear holding a bear cub. The cub, speared through by Romonon's spear, lay motionless in the dark of the night.

The prince — unaware — for the bears whose growls had so joyously greeted him before, were now silenced with grief, so he climbed back up the rock. As he did so, behind him, the speared carcass of a peacock, another of a fish and one of a rabbit washed past the buried crystal. That night, a deep red colour flowed in Elvador that the shepherd had not seen flowing there before.

Harry finished his story, then dropped to his knees, looking at Othelia desperately with tears in his eyes, clasping his abdomen in pain.

"It hurts me, Othelia," he gasped. "It hurts me so much."

The little girl was sobbing already. Unable to see her friend in pain, she slid off the tree trunk and put her arms around him and they cried together for a while, until it seemed as though the secret garden started to swirl around them and suddenly, they had been transported to Elvador again, both crouching, arms around one another, by the stream.

There, the chirpy bird that had chatted to them earlier sat cocking its head this way and that, on what looked like a cut block of ice that projected up from the shore of the stream. A fish swam by, stopping to look at its reflection in the bird's crystal pedestal.

The tears were cleared from the eyes of Othelia and Harry and they turned to see what it was that growled behind them.

Four bears frolicked there, in front of the cave — two parent bears overjoyed at watching their twin cubs play and the two cubs overjoyed for no reason in particular.

Three pochal trees stood between the bears and the two children.

Othelia looked on in wonder, while Harry's eyes met those of the mother and father bears, as they stopped bouncing around their cubs to look soulfully at Harry.

Harry, his eyes filled again with tears, looked back at the mother and father bears helplessly, as though the sorrow of a lifetime had seared through him.

Mother bear, affection for the two small children playing in her heart (for she had two small children of her own), listened knowingly as father bear began to growl again. How Othelia and Harry understood what he wished to convey was unclear, but understand the bear they did.

"The prince shared our sorrow," the bear began, "and thus carried our burden for us when we could not bear it alone. His love, agony and heartfelt wishes projected into this universe like a prayer and resurrected our son. Our prince has become our king in doing so. His only wish was to ever help us."

Tears rolled down Harry's face as he listened to the bear and little Othelia again put her arms about her sweet friend to hold him while the emotions rushed through him.

"Look Harry," she said, gently, wiping his tears and cupping his cheek. "The little bear is alive. So is the fish. There are animals here in Elvador. No more hunting." she shook her head to assure him that the problem was no more.

A rabbit hopped by their feet. The mother and father bears growled in laughter, the cubs wrestled tirelessly and a peacock, high above on the rock, danced a portrait of colours with its feathers.

Elvador began to spin around them and suddenly, Othelia and Harry were back in the secret garden.

Harry turned to Othelia and took her little hands into his own (which were not much bigger). Tears still clinging to his eyes, he looked at her and said, "You see, Othelia — one day, all things that ever went wrong… are put right."

When Othelia left the secret garden, she left a happy Harry.

She ran back through the other gardens of the house, losing the bow in her hair on the way, arriving back at the kitchen with rosy cheeks. Her father strode into the kitchen and already pleased, was further delighted to find his daughter there, looking like she had been invigorated by all that nature had to offer.

Today was special indeed, for many long-awaited

revisions had been made for the benefit of the land and its creatures. The businessmen farmers, blessed with caring and a love of the land and all that lived on it, had pushed aside the traditions of their forefathers for new visions to light up existence in its many forms.

"Today is a special occasion." Othelia's father voiced his thoughts to the little girl as she ran to him to wrap her arms around his legs.

He ruffled her hair, then went over to the fruit bowl to pick up the jar hidden by it.

Othelia stood back sharply, pursing her lips to look at him in worried anticipation.

Othelia's father held the jar of marble-like sweeties to the light, frowned for a moment and then looked at his daughter with an amused expression.

"Would you like a sweetie, my darling?" he asked.

Othelia relaxed and drew closer to inspect the jar as her father held it towards her. There were no blue-coloured sweets in the jar; nor were there crimson ones, lilac ones, green ones, golden ones or orange ones with hues of pink through them. There were only brown sweets, cream-coloured sweets and some black ones in the jar.

"No thank you, Daddy," Othelia refused politely, as her father suppressed a smile. He knew that she was sweetened enough already.

Othelia's mother appeared at the door of the kitchen and exclaimed, "Othelia, my darling — you're here! Did you have a good play, my love?"

As ever, there was no time for Othelia to answer the questions. The satchel was removed from her shoulders and she was swooped into her mother's arms and carried upstairs to be dressed for an outing that had been planned.

Yeela, the stranger-lady of gems who had once visited the household at a time of dilemma, was holding a seminar at a hall in the central square of the city. She was much revered and though she was rarely seen publicly, any event she initiated was well attended by the people of the city. She was a wise lady and people were keen to absorb her guidance.

This day, she spoke of the rainbow of colours that healed. Violet for the mind, blue for expression, green for the heart, gold for happiness, orange for hope and crimson for passions and grounding.

At the end of the seminar, Othelia (having neither listened to, nor understood most of Yeela's talk) followed her mother to a table, upon which there were various artefacts displayed for purchase. Othelia's mother immediately spied a small bracelet of gem beads of different colours and grasped it excitedly to show Othelia.

"For you, my darling!" she informed her little daughter, with enthusiasm.

Othelia squeezed through the women who were gathering round the table to look, for herself, at the wares laid there. Standing on tiptoes, she surveyed the table and saw on it a spiral pendant-holder, suspended from a chain that was within her reach. She stretched forward, wrapped the chain around her little fingers and lifted it for her mother to see.

Puzzled, her mother gazed at the empty holder and gave Othelia a questioning look.

"I have something to put in it, Mummy," the little girl explained.

Her mother laughed, unwinding the chain from Othelia's fingers.

"What could you possibly have to put in it?" she asked Othelia, more a question for herself in surprise at what the small girl was capable of thinking of. "I don't even know what this thing is myself!"

A lady behind the table snapped the spiral open to explain to Othelia's mother that a crystal could be placed within. Two presents were thus bought for Othelia.

Once back in the house, Othelia ran up to her room to retrieve the crystal Yeela had left her and brought it downstairs so that her mother could make a pendant of it. Her mother did so, joyfully perplexed at her daughter's request, wondering where the crystal had come from. Once the chain with the clear crystal was locked into the spiral holder and hung around Othelia's neck, her gentle mother also fixed the colourful, gem bracelet onto Othelia's wrist.

Othelia toyed with the bracelet, seeing that each of the gem beads were the colour of a missing shade of sweetie from the hidden sweetie jar. She touched the beads one by one and each reminded her of the feeling and taste the corresponding sweet had infused her with: blue, lilac, green, golden, orange-pink...

Thankfully, before she could touch the crimson, ruby bead, her mother swept her daughter's hand into her own to take the little girl upstairs and tuck her into bed.

Zohor

Othelia's delicate mother had been unwell for days. Othelia's father had cancelled many a pressing appointment of late, dark shadows haunting his eyes with worry. Othelia would hear him in the early mornings, escorting his fevered wife to the bathroom, where she would inevitably be sick.

Othelia would clutch the edge of her comforter, only her eyes peeping from it, as she lay in bed, unable to penetrate the aura surrounding her parents, much as she wanted to. It was as though an invisible force held them from her.

A faithful friend of her mother's — Tomari — had arrived at the house a day after the sickness had begun. Well-meaning, but different to Othelia's mother, Tomari formed a practical substitute, feeding Othelia and keeping the little girl occupied. As ever, the grown-ups had forgotten to inform the child as to what it was exactly that had changed the atmosphere so.

Othelia did not mind, but if she had stopped to think about it, she would have noticed that she found it harder to breathe in this period and sometimes she took several breaths in quick succession, as though after a long cry.

Ten days into the episode, a humour interrupted Othelia's mother's sickness. Bedridden as she was, her gentle smile was back and she lay, somewhat strengthened, in the sunshine that shone through the open windows of the bedroom. She asked for Othelia — her first thought as she was delivered from delirium.

Othelia, held at the shoulders by a smiling Tomari, hesitated at the doorway of her mother's bedroom. She, too, looked thinner like her mother, but two bows decorated her hair in bunches either side of her head.

Tomari left to go and finish preparing lunch and Othelia's mother sat up slightly, holding her arms out to Othelia in beckoning delight.

Othelia went over to her mother's arms and greeted her, "Hello, Mummy," as her mother pulled her onto the bed to lay down with her — she, under the covers and Othelia above them, looking like a pair of Russian dolls.

"Mummy, are you not well?" Othelia asked, turning to look at her mother, cupping one little hand against her mother's soft cheek.

"I am much better now that you are here." Othelia's mother beamed, squeezing the little girl in a tight cuddle.

"Mummy, I went to look for Harry, but I couldn't find him today," Othelia related. "I wanted to give him something to eat — he's very thin," she concluded, nodding at her appraisal of her leaf-clad friend.

Othelia's mother smiled to herself, ever amazed at the little girl's imagination. This invisible character, Harry, seemed to be many things and now he was thinner too!

"What does he normally eat?" she asked Othelia, who was playing with tassels on the bedcover now.

"Pochals, Mummy! But not all the time. Only when he goes to Elvador."

"Pochals?" Othelia's mother turned Othelia to look at her most interestedly. "Like in the dancing girl's story?"

"Yes, Mummy, the shepherd planted them."

"The shepherd? Oh yes." Othelia's mother humoured her child. "The dancing girl sent him seeds, didn't she? And do you eat pochals, too, when you're with Harry?" she queried.

"Yes, Mummy — but only one time. The bears were there the second time and we didn't eat pochals then."

Bears. Her little daughter would never fail to surprise her, thought Othelia's mother.

"And what do pochals taste like?" she asked, for surely there was an answer to this, too.

Othelia giggled until her cheeks were rosy and said, "They taste very nice."

Her mother tickled her to fuel the giggling and such games ensued until the two girls fell asleep — one through exhaustion and the onset of another fever and the other relaxed by the comfort of her mother's arms.

Othelia drifted into dreamland, where Zohor, in its many colours, re-played a scene from its history.

***

In the prince's eighteenth year, on his return from Elvador, he found his father, Orion, taken sick by a purging illness that left the old king fevered and bedbound.

"My Prince," he would say feebly to his son, when the boy visited him at his bedside, "you must visit my people and do what you can for them until I am strong enough to bring you into your powers."

The young prince only understood some of what his fevered father told him and carried that out with the zeal of Orion himself.

Ambassadors, though they visited the palace, were

informed only that their wise king was too sickly to help them and soon the word spread throughout Zohor and mass-praying began across the land to bring the beloved king back into health.

Word reached Elvador soon after the king's illness began, as a postman was despatched to carry a portrait-sized version of the stamp of the shepherd to the nature-loving artist who tended sheep on the pastures.

"Our King is sick," the postman informed the shepherd.

The shepherd, heartbroken already at a devastating observation that animals had been killed and were disappearing in Elvador, was saddened further. He consequently went to call upon the lavender-growing ambassador of Elvador; the ambassador was preparing himself for a journey to the palace, to ask for help regarding the animals.

The shepherd, portrait in hand, knocked on the door of the ambassador's wooden abode that resembled a doll's house; it stood almost precariously near the edge of a rock-flat overlooking fields of lavender.

The shepherd knocked softly. The door was ajar, showing a bustling ambassador packing a bag, while his small daughter gaily skipped about him, singing a new-found rhyme over and over.

On hearing the knock, the ambassador stopped packing, placed a hand on his frolicking daughter's head to steady her, then flung the door open to welcome his visitor.

A look of shock crossed his face when he was met with the sight of the forlorn, young shepherd leaning against the door frame, as though he could not have stood without its support.

"My son!" the ambassador said, transferring his hand from his daughter's head to the shepherd's shoulder. "What ails you?"

"It is not I," the shepherd replied, emotion filling his eyes. "It is our King who is sick. Your journey will be a wasted one if you choose to make it."

The ambassador helped the shepherd into the house and seated him in a wooden chair, while the little, playful girl eyed the shepherd's portrait inquisitively. She stepped forward and touched the embossed surface with her fingers, feeling the urge to sing again.

Her father, sensing the signs, lifted his daughter away from the portrait and called to his wife, "Ria!"

A plump, aproned lady appeared from the kitchen and instinctively held her hands out to receive the child.

"Oh, hello dear," she said to the shepherd. "Would you like some barley drink? I have agave nectar to put in it."

She put her fingers against the shepherd's cheek to lift his downcast face and looked at him with concern.

"Will you take Sayra into the kitchen, love?" her husband asked her.

She gave him a look that said she understood and carried the child, whose energies were beginning to vocalise again, into the kitchen.

The ambassador sat down opposite the shepherd.

"Perhaps I could take him some lavender," he said. "I feel, in my heart, that an interesting subspecies I have been growing can aid ailments of a variety. Perhaps it is our turn to help our King?"

The shepherd looked at him sadly.

"But you cannot now tell him of the plight of our

animals," he said to the ambassador. "That would only make him more ill with perplexion."

"My son," the ambassador looked at the young man, wisely, "we can but deal with one problem at a time. Perhaps my journey is destined — but for a different purpose to what we thought. Only the king can stop the disappearance of animals from Elvador. Perhaps we have to save him first."

And so, the ambassador for Elvador set off on a long journey to the City of the Palace, supported by a kiss goodbye on his right cheek from Sayra and one on his left from Ria.

Two weeks later, as the shepherd looked at the new centrepiece in his living room — a portrait of himself — the postman visited once again: this time, with a packet from Melthon. Anonymous, it contained three seeds, with a request for planting. The animals were leaving Elvador, the shepherd thought. Perhaps the planting of seeds from afar could rejuvenate life in Elvador...

The ambassador of Elvador arrived eventually at the palace. His horse was weary from the journey and the packets of lavender in his bag less fresh than when he had set out. The peoples he had met along the way had been ever welcoming, observing their duties to the ambassadors, for they would always wish their own ambassadors to be treated with welcome on their journeys, too.

"Our King is sick, sire. He will not be able to help you at present," the ambassador of the palace informed his counterpart from Elvador.

"I seek not his help, fair messenger — I am here to offer mine," the ambassador from Elvador explained.

The old queen, keen to hear of anything that could heal her husband, arranged rest for the visitor from Elvador in a little-used room at the palace, that offered a plush comfort of velvet cushions of deep green, outside which grew a herb garden that she, herself, tended to.

The next morning, she met with the rested ambassador, who was overjoyed to spend time with the legendary queen, whose beauty as a young woman had enchanted Zohor. He understood now that the deep beauty of the young prince he had met not long before sprouted from deeply beautiful roots. Orion was famed for his healing influence and loving advice over all the kingdom, but just one look at the queen was a healing influence of its own.

"Ambassador, you bring us help in our time of need — and that too, from the very herbs that speak to my heart so," she said to Elvador's man of lavender. "Did you sleep well, dear friend? Did you enjoy the view of the garden from your window?" Her eyes sparkled as they had done at the age of eighteen, when she had planted the garden outside the room she had decorated, in the hope of sleeping a royal child there.

As it had turned out, when the young prince had eventually been born, he was much too delicate for her to sleep him in the almost forgotten room. He had slept, as a baby, in a cot by his mother's bedside, so that when either of them awoke at night, a companion was there to drive away night-time worries. As a child, the young prince had been moved to a room with a skylight, many windows and a view of the woodland. The room was beside the top half of the king's magical room of mystery; the king had deemed its proximity a good thing to help the health of the little boy.

And so, the queen's room by the herb garden had forever remained empty, like an unblossomed flower.

Elvador's ambassador told the queen he had much

enjoyed the view from the room.

"You grow many magical herbs there, my Queen." he smiled at her, his eyes sparkling, too, as he looked into those of the kindred spirit before him. "A catalogue of them would be of most interest to a man like me."

He laid out, on a small table that stood between them, two varieties of lavender — one that was common to Zohor and another which the queen had not encountered before. The dark leaves of the latter, almost shaped like insects' wings, enticed her to squeeze one between her fingers to release its aroma. A eucalyptic blend of medicinal and fragrant infusion burst into the air and the old queen gasped in surprise; she sat back in her chair and looked as though two decades had escaped her.

"My Queen," said the ambassador of Elvador, "this may help our King."

And so, a programme was drawn up to bring regular quantities of the herb from the pastures of Elvador to the City of the Palace. Bowls of the herb were placed about the sickly king's bedroom; aromatic oils from it were applied to his forehead and even a light tea of it was fed gently to him by the hands of his queen.

Two weeks into the treatment, the king slowly showed a response mustering in him. His ailing and almost lifeless face shot an unexpected, mischievous smile at the queen as she administered his tea one morning.

Elvador remained devoid of animals, but this information was kept a secret and for one full year, the ambassador of Elvador journeyed regularly to bring packets of his loving crop to the palace. The postman who visited Elvador was sworn, too, to secrecy, such that word of the problem would not worry the royal household in their time of need.

71

No wool was taken to the markets of Zohor from Elvador that year. The people of Zohor, ever respectful, knew of the ambassador of Elvador's labour of love that was helping their king and trusted that if no reason had been given for the absence of the wool, then that was reason good enough.

One day, after suffering his illness for a year, the old king sat up in bed with colour in his cheeks, just in time to receive the young prince returning from his trip to Melthon.

The young prince hastened to his father's bedroom on his arrival. Throughout the old king's illness, Prince Thallon had carried out his princely duties with zeal, reporting back to his father's bedside, convinced that the accounts he gave would spur his father into getting better. Already there flew a feeling in his heart lighter than he had ever known, on his journey back from Melthon; to find his father well, served to consolidate the joy that spread through his being.

On the day the old king felt fit and well enough to dress himself, the ambassador from Elvador arrived with his last packet of potent lavender. The old queen met him by clasping his hands into hers, for he had, indeed, become a dear friend. On this occasion, the ambassador brought with him one further packet — specifically for the queen and an envelope intended for the king on his recovery.

The old queen took her friend to the herb garden.

"Why don't you open the packet I have brought for you, my Queen?" the ambassador asked her.

Inside the wrapped, sealed packet, Queen Nelatron found seeds, gladly harvested by the ambassador from his one special field that grew the lavender that had sustained the old king.

"I do not know that they will grow so well, here, ambassador," the old queen told him, understanding that these were seeds from which would spring the eucalyptic, purple healer. "These are not the rich pastures of Elvador."

"But they have your hands to grow them," the ambassador reassured his queen gently, laying kind hands over hers, in encouragement.

The ambassador of Elvador was sent that time from the City of the Palace, with a large celebration which the king himself attended.

"What may I do for you to thank you, gentle ambassador?" the old king asked the celebrated man before his departure.

The ambassador handed him the envelope containing information that had been suppressed in Elvador, daily breaking the young shepherd's heart for a year.

After the departure of her ambassador friend, the old queen, having seen to it that her newly enlivened husband was resting to preserve his health, climbed down the palace stairway and headed towards the plush room she had once decorated in such hope. She had asked her ever-attentive maids for some privacy for her thoughts, but they followed her a little of the way, with looks of concern on their faces.

Once in the room, the queen stood by the window, looking at the garden that twinkled with health outside. A small, bare patch, newly tilled, anticipated the sprouting of a gift from Elvador.

Her husband was well again — a result of the very medicinal herbs she had so been in love with all her life.

Her king was a kindly man and attended to all his kingdom commendably. She had supported him in his mission from the time he had been a prince of Thallon's age. Many a sacrifice she had endured to ensure that the king's duties were conducted undisturbed. She remembered the time of Thallon's long-awaited birth, when Orion had been deeply spent in solving the seemingly urgent problems of one of the regions of Zohor. His diligence meant that he had missed the birth of his precious son. Such sacrifices were commonplace to royalty, but a queen's heart is still that of a woman's…

Standing by the window in the plush room, old queen Nelatron remembered that, as a young woman, she would touch the leaves of the herbs in the garden outside and become infused with a sense of the sweet purpose of each one. Coriander would give her a sense of super-nourishment, its delicate leaves ready to offer the touch of femininity to anything they decorated. Mint, with its desire to refresh everything would make her laugh — so amicable was the herb that it felt like a good friend. For it was not only the king in the royal household who was gifted with insight: Prince Thallon was born of two magical people.

The queen looked lovingly at the garden, breathing in the aromas of the herbs through the open window. Inspired, she left the windowsill to walk over to a wooden dresser, that sat by a wall in the room. She opened a small drawer at the top of the dresser and drew from it a book of empty pages, bound in an embroidered, gilded cover.

She had acquired it many years ago — a gift from her doting father — to record her dreams and her progress in. She had thought she would write and sketch in it while a baby slept in the room, but it had never been used, as she had forgotten about it by the time of young Thallon's arrival (and he had never slept in that room, anyway).

With a smile, Queen Nelatron settled amongst some plump cushions and opened the book.

On the first page, she wrote, "For my dear friend, the ambassador of Elvador." And on the second, in large writing, "The Book of Herbs."

She thought she would include in it a particular chapter about lavender, to educate aspiring herb-growers on the potent properties of the plant.

In the herb garden outside, the memory of a young princess of startling beauty fingered her plants in delight, her heart potent with dreams.

Inside the room, the old queen thought for a moment, as she began to write accounts of her herbs, that her king had never seen the herb garden. She hoped young Thallon would, when he found a princess of his own, take much joy in his princess' passions.

In a far off Elvador, to where the queen's friend the ambassador travelled, three small plants could be seen sprouting in a soil they had not encountered before, in front of a cave, behind a rock...

One gloriously sunny day, soon after the old king's recovery, while the people, plants and objects of Zohor were splashed by the happiness of Paolon and Safera, King Orion took his son, the young Prince Thallon, into the gardens of the palace to bestow upon him a most important procedure.

In the moments of clarity during his illness, the old king had recognised that the time had come for younger blood to take rule over Zohor.

"My son," he said to his object of much affection, who walked obediently by him, through gardens of the most incredible flowers and walkways, planted and cut by the inspired gardeners of the palace. "My magic is not one that is innate."

He looked at the boy to assess a reaction. The young prince met his father's gaze steadily, prepared for whatever his father was about to tell him.

"Zohor and all the other planets of this Universe and beyond are governed by a force which speaks to us through the blossoms of our land." The king cupped a golden dahlia in one hand. "The kindness of a heart, the beauty of a woman's eyes, the nourishment of the fruit from trees…"

The old king gestured about him as he spoke, to indicate the whereabouts of the phenomena, he spoke of.

"There are powers and laws we have forgotten, encased as we are in bodies of flesh — so delightful as to allow us experience, but vulnerable for they act as filters."

"Filters to what, father?" the prince asked, kneeling to offer his hand to a bird that was perched on the ground between them, looking inquisitively from one royal to the other.

"Our senses are filters, my son," the king elaborated. "Our skin — a filter to feeling; our ears — filters to hearing; our sight — a filter to seeing…" He paused.

The bird listened on with its princely, fellow student.

"It is time for you to see and hear and feel things your eyes and ears and skin do not allow you to," the king continued, with a smile included for the bird.

The young prince stood up, feeling this to be appropriate and the bird arranged itself in line with the prince to face the king accordingly.

"My son, it is my duty to attune you, such that you may sense the things I do," the king revealed.

The prince drew a breath, knowing it would be one of his last as a prince.

"When you place your hands upon things, you will be able

to heal them and will understand their ailment with clairvoyance, clairaudience and the feelings of others and our fellow creations in this Universe."

The bird stood ready.

The king sat his son under a tree that cast a canopy of protection from the unblemished rays of Paolon and Safera, for there would be enough light filling him shortly and a being of flesh is only designed to sustain a limited current of light. The prince's companion bird settled by him under the tree.

The prince closed his eyes, as asked to by his father and King Orion attuned the boy for a channel to permeate though him — a vortex, through which the wisdom of the Universe could make itself known to the young man.

Bird and prince alike saw visions of existences that had long escaped them. They viewed lights of the rainbow of creation and connected to ancestors, who had long-awaited visiting rights to communicate with them.

The prince came round from the attunement an hour later, feeling a distinct warmth in his hands.

The bird, happy to have spent time with royalty, flew off to do birdly things of equal importance.

The prince looked up at his father, who stood smiling benevolently at the young, rather startled man, holding a glass bottle of water out to him.

The prince took the water, drank it thirstily and accepted some nuts and dried fruit his father also pulled out from within his large, pocketed sleeve.

Sitting by the prince, the king looked at his son with a slight mischief before briefing the boy on the new gifts that had been bestowed upon him.

At the end, the old king said, "Let us give it some time for you to become accustomed to the new energies and I shall then make a teacher of you, too. There is much to learn of cosmic energy. Our little planet with its tiny land space, is but one of many, all governed by the same force of creation that runs through each and every one of us. What we do influences the others as what they do influences us. That is why we must do our best — for the good of all."

With that, the kindly, old king (for the first time since the prince was a child) helped his son up from the ground and the two gentlemen returned to the world where they were met by courtiers and concerned attendants, whose thoughts forever supported their royal charges, even in moments of stolen privacy.

The following week, the king requested a third throne to be placed by his in the main court. This day, the ambassador of Melthon was visitor to the palace, carrying a question sent by the alchemist of the village of berries.

The young prince, seated for the first time in a throne by his parents, blushed a smile at the ambassador of Melthon, for he held fresh memories of the village of berries and its inhabitants — one in particular — in his heart.

The ambassador of Melthon raised an eyebrow at the prince, partly with amusement that the young boy was now holding court and partly through pride that Melthon's charming, recent, young visitor had graduated so in the short time since his visit.

"You bring us a question?" the king asked the ambassador gently, pleased to be healthy and fit to resume his duties. "How has Melthon fared in my absence?"

"Melthon has fared well to have been so recently blessed by the presence of our prince, my King," the ambassador reported. He enquired after the king's health, expressing his delight at the king's recovery, before drawing a bracelet of gems of various colours from a velvet pouch.

The young prince drew a startled breath, which thankfully went unnoticed in the background rumble of the court agreeing with the ambassador's happiness about the return of their king.

The young prince gripped the armrests of his throne such that his fingers sunk deep into the cushioned padding and steeled himself, barely blinking and hoping the sound of his pounding heart could not be heard echoing around the court.

"My King," the ambassador said, holding the bracelet before him, "the alchemist of Melthon sends me. Eighteen years and two months ago, Melthon was blessed by the birth of a divine child, whose energies have illuminated our village since her birth. She is the alchemist's daughter, Maria."

Prince Thallon shut his eyes as a feeling that had been his constant companion since meeting the dancing girl suddenly coursed through him, threatening to break its boundaries and overflow.

The gem bracelet was passed up to the old king.

"Ambassador," the king smiled, "I am an old man and have guided Zohor for many a year. The honesty of my people has been the basis of my work and now, I must be honest with you."

The old king looked around the court, so as to address not just the visitor from Melthon, but all who were present. His eyes finally settled upon his queen by his side and they smiled reassurance to one another, before the old king turned to speak to the ambassador of Melthon once more.

"Good man, I propose that your prince now guides you."

The prince opened his eyes and turned to look at his father.

There was silence in the court.

The king met his son's look, smiled once more, reached over to take the young prince's hand and folded the bracelet into it.

"What is your query, ambassador?" the king turned to ask Melthon's spokesman.

"My King... my Prince," the ambassador began, flustered to have witnessed and participated in such a monumental and historic moment. "The people of Melthon are good people — people of nature and clean of heart. We are not... people of magic. The alchemist, who works with the elements to transform them, has transformed our blood to magic in Maria. The young lads of our village are kindly, but simple. The alchemist sends me to ask you for guidance on a suitor for Maria."

"Then this will be your first task in guiding the people of Zohor," the king said, turning to look at the prince once more.

The old king reached into the folds of his mantle and drew out the envelope given to him by the ambassador of Elvador. He held it out to the prince, saying, "And this will be your second."

Court concluded that day with a bewildered prince leaving the first sitting of his throne. Despatched to the magical room for the first time on his own, he walked gingerly, clutching the bracelet that had danced so often in his mind in one hand and the letter from Elvador in the other.

The bracelet, infused with the energies of the dancing girl, caused him to catch his breath as he entered the room. The young prince closed the door, threw his back to it and stood there, eyes shut, breathing deep lungfuls, his iron-tight fists jammed against the door either side of him to steady him, clutching their objects.

Eventually, he raised his head to look at the skylight, high above, in the centre of the room. Paolon and Safera with their unwavering beams seemed unaffected by the tumult that swirled inside the prince. A suitor for the dancing girl. It was his job to see.

In another part of the palace, towards a plush room overlooking a herb garden, an old king with the heart of a young man walked to follow the young girl he had met and fallen in love with so many years ago.

After his illness, he had visited his magical room of wisdom and mystery one final time, where he had been told his work was done. And so, he had asked one last question, for the first time — guidance for himself. He had then been shown a vision of his bride princess, planting herbs with zeal and decorating a room, overjoyed with the excitement that he would come and see what she had done. Tears had sprung to his eyes, as he watched the vision progress to show his lovely bride's inspirations dampened and her heart feel a blow whenever his calls to duty had drawn him away from her.

His last moments in the magical room had seen him crumpled, sobbing. For he had been a kind king, a wise king and had fulfilled the duties of his tradition. But to have hurt the heart of the woman he loved made him less than a king and not even worthy to be a man.

His job was done. Free, he had but one desire.

He had warded off his attendants after the court session and having seen his queen do the same moments earlier, he followed her softly, his heart breaking with each step as hers would have done over him a thousand times, as she had stood by and supported him. He had not had the strength to ask of the Wisdom in the magic room, "Why did you fail to show me?" For he knew that the love in his heart should have guided him.

He approached the door of the plush room, not knowing what he would find inside. The outside of the door, painted green, seemed as though it was fit for young Thallon. The old king, feeling much as he had done when he had first approached the gardener of Dalatur's daughter, Nelatron, tapped the door with a trembling knuckle. So beautiful she had been that he, as a young prince, would have done anything for her. His whole existence would have felt as though he had been swinging from the stars if she would but take notice of him. He knew in his heart it was his duty to look after her — to make her smile the way she lit his heart up...

The green door opened slowly to reveal Queen Nelatron, her eyes flowing with inspiration, mingled with a hint of curiosity as to who might be chapping at her door.

The sight of the king trembling helplessly in the doorway was the last thing she had expected to see.

"Forgive me," he said.

"For what, my darling?" she asked him, taking his hands into her own and drawing him into the room.

"For not understanding. You are my strength. You are my reason for being. There is no moment that has magic for me if you are not there."

The queen stopped and stood still, looking at her husband, hardly able to believe her ears.

"I have been there for everyone," the king continued, his lips quivering as he spoke. He looked down, shook his head and looked back up at his queen. "But I have not been there for you."

The queen's expression softened to the utmost compassion, as she raised her hands to cup her husband's face.

"You had no choice," she said, her eyes, too, filling with tears now. "You did what you had to do. If you had lived and breathed your love for me, you could not have been the King of Zohor. I understand that. We have both made our sacrifices for our people. It was our job to — there was no other way. They are my people, too."

The king cried some more, his heart cracking open to fall into the lap of she who was his strength.

Sometime later, the king and queen, free of their mantles, looked together excitedly at The Book of Herbs, before going into the herb garden, where the king fingered the leaves of the herbs, learning of their wisdom from his wife. At the end of the tour of the garden, the king, looking years younger, stood viewing a bare patch in the soil. He knelt by the patch and looked up at his queen, who also seemed to look younger.

"And what is it you grow here, my darling?" he asked, as the beautiful lady came to kneel by him.

"Lavender, my Prince," she whispered softly to him, running her finger down his cheek. "It's the reason you are here…"

***

Othelia awoke from her sleep to feel her mother's cheek burning against hers. Soft moans emanated from the fevered lady as she, too, came round from a sleep. Hers, unlike her daughter's, had been fraught with perilous dreams.

Tomari, who had previously checked on the sleeping girls, arrived again at the door of the bedroom, promptly in time to hear pained coughs perturbing Othelia's mother.

Othelia turned round to hold her mother's face in her little hands.

"Mummy," she said, emotion welling inside her.

Tomari walked over to the bed, lifted Othelia into her arms and then placed the little girl to stand on the floor.

"Will you fetch your father?" she asked, gently.

Othelia ran off to find her father, while Tomari assessed her friend's situation.

Downstairs, Othelia found her father in his study, his head hung between his hands, looking at some papers on his desk.

"Daddy!" Othelia called, running up to him. "Mummy's unwell again."

Her father took his hands down from his face and looked at his daughter. The premature creases on his face had deepened and his complexion was grey with worry.

As he carried her back upstairs, Othelia, desperate to help, suggested to her father, "Perhaps lavender would help, Daddy?"

But her father, consumed by the thought of his beloved wife's illness, heard only the moans that flowed out to him from the bedroom.

The Melting Pot

Othelia's mother had recovered somewhat from her illness, although her skin looked thin and clung to the bones of her face, leaving hollows around her eyes. The sickness continued in less frequent bursts, but she was now able to eat small portions from time to time, to compensate a little for her loss of vitality.

The fever, on occasion, still visited and sometimes she would clutch her belly in pain for a short while before steeling herself with determination and resuming some chore or another.

Today, she was cooking something in a large pot that resembled a vessel a witch might use. It was the first time Othelia's mother had cooked since the onset of the illness. She had drawn her hair back sharply from her face and wore a lace shawl about her shoulders, tucked in by her elbows. She gathered ingredients, adding them one by one and peering into the pot with an expression of, "What should I put in?" after each addition.

She knew her husband would not be pleased to learn of her activities when he returned from his duties that day — he had arranged for food to be cooked and brought to them each day and some home-help to see to the household until she was better. But Othelia's mother had a life to live, whatever her condition, and today she felt like cooking something magical for her family.

"Othelia, my darling," she said, holding her index finger stretched in the air, a remnant of the delirium of illness still playing in her demeanour.

Othelia slid off a kitchen chair, where she had been sitting, painting a picture at the table.

"Yes, Mummy?" she asked, drawing up to her mother, who stood looking like the ghost of a schoolteacher, softened by drapes of lace.

"The magic is in the blending," her mother continued. "Potatoes without salt are incomplete," she explained, retrieving a small piece of potato from the pot, blowing on it to cool it, dusting it with a few grains of salt and popping it into Othelia's mouth.

Othelia ate it happily, wrapping her arms round her mother's legs, savouring the complement of sharp salt with soft potato.

Her mother retrieved a piece of potato for herself, also, finding her appetite to be alive all of a sudden. She continued to merge flavours into one another in the pot, until she was satisfied they had melted together, to form a delicious taste of novel combination.

A gentle knock at the open door of the kitchen revealed the smiling face of the postman. Othelia ran over to him: the postman was a kindly man who carried toffees for the children of the houses he delivered mail to. He pretended not to notice Othelia, smiling directly at her mother, instead, asking after her well-being.

Othelia's mother, in return, retrieved a piece of potato for the postman.

Othelia skipped around in front of the postman's legs,

periodically calling to him for his attention. He continued to ignore her and she giggled, as this was often his game — to tease her, as though to make her work for her reward. She stopped skipping and thought, perhaps, that offering her painting to him would get him to notice her. The acknowledgement of his kindly eyes was almost as sweet as the toffees he brought.

"Mr Postman," Othelia said, dragging the painting off the table and taking it to him, "I painted a picture for you."

She stood and held it in front of herself for him to see.

This appeared to do the trick. He stopped enquiring after her mother's health and looked at the painting silently, instead, squinting his face and surveying it with some judgement.

"Hmm," he said, eventually, "there is something about the painting that suggests... that suggests it was not painted for me!"

Othelia burst into giggles and the postman reached into his satchel, bringing out two toffees — one with orange wrapping and one with green.

"Mr Postman," Othelia said, "you can have the painting."

"Well, that, I think, is a very fair trade," said the postman with twinkling eyes, as they exchanged goods. The postman had no children of his own and any reminder of how much the children of the neighbourhood adored him was a source of great joy on lonely days.

He handed a newspaper to Othelia's mother, who had come over and was brushing locks of hair from Othelia's forehead, tucking them round the back of small ears, behind which was tied a rainbow-coloured bow.

"Ma'am, I wish you good health," the postman nodded, taking his leave.

87

The pot on the stove was boiling vigorously, but Othelia's mother forgot about it for a while, as she caught sight of an unusual headline in the newspaper:

ANIMALS AND POCHALS IN ELVADOR

Elvador — one of the far-off areas her husband's committee was responsible for. Since the time of King Orion, no animals had ever been seen in Elvador. The fields, wasted by the industrial farming of times gone, had lain uninhabited and largely unvisited for many a year. And pochals? These were the mythical fruits spoken of in secret documentaries written by the legendary Prince Thallon. No one in the modern world had ever seen one and for the most part, they were regarded as a fantasy.

Elvador had many trees — all peculiar to that particular region. Nothing — to date — could have identified the tree of the pochal. Apparently, now, three trees previously undocumented as fruit-bearing had been found to be producing fruit that fitted the description of the mythical pochals. Even visits by explorers to long-demolished Melthon had only uncovered three dead trees in an enclosure of withered woodland that may have formed the famed orchard of the prince's story.

Othelia's mother absorbed the article. After the meeting of the businessmen farmers at her home, a delegate had been despatched to assess the condition of deserted Elvador, such that plans could be made to revive the once rich area. The newspaper reported that the delegate (a young, artistic man, with a passion for all things in nature) had arrived with a colleague to find Elvador populated, once more, with the very animals described by Prince Thallon in the era of Orion. Notably, a family of bears was found to be living in the caves again and it was in front of these that the mysterious trees bearing large, berry-like fruit grew.

Othelia's mother's head began to spin as the pot behind her bubbled. What was it her daughter had said to her that day, just before the fever? Her head spun until she felt too dizzy to stand and the sudden prick of a chill at the back of her neck sent a shudder through her.

"Othelia," she gasped, steadying herself by holding onto a chair.

The newspaper dropped to the floor.

Othelia, oblivious, had gone upstairs carrying toffees in her mouth, to find her crystal pendant she felt inspired to wear. Mummy would put it on for her. She pulled it from a box in which she kept trinkets of interest to her — buttons, rocks and a small portrait of her mother, set in a gilded frame.

Already affected by the sugar in the toffees, she skipped back downstairs to ask for her mother's assistance with the crystal necklace.

She skipped into the kitchen at speed and ran to put her arms around her mother's skirt, as the frail lady stood gripping the chair.

Her mother felt hot.

Othelia drew her head back to look up at her mother who was surprisingly silent.

"Mummy…" she ventured, to stir her mother from her statuesque pose.

Othelia's mother, a fever riding up her back once more, moved forward clutching her daughter with one hand and the table with the other and pulled herself into the chair.

"Othelia, my darling," her voice was breathless, as she tried desperately to keep her thoughts clear from the delirium that was already clouding. "Tell me again, about Elvador. How many pochal trees did you see there?"

"Mummy," Othelia responded, still holding the crystal pendant and glad now that her mother was speaking again, "there are three trees."

"Where?"

"In front of where the bears live. Harry likes the bears."

"What does he look like — Harry?"

"Mummy, sometimes he doesn't look so happy. Sometimes his leaves change colour."

"His leaves?"

"He wears leaves — green ones. And a flower cap on his head. But he wouldn't let me tell him about the dancing girl, Mummy. That made me upset. I thought he would like her very much."

Around Othelia's little wrist, held in her mother's hand, was the bracelet of gems that had been bought after the businessmen's meeting.

The pot on the stove had cooked its contents now — the different flavours blended to give one.

In Othelia's mother's mind, the delirium mixed with reality and for a few moments, she saw clearly — through time — to fit together jigsaw pieces that were eras apart, to form one picture.

"Darling," she said, knowing she was soon to collapse, "why don't you go and tell him about the dancing girl now? Mummy will finish making dinner."

Othelia looked at her mother for a moment, hesitating, but — forever an obedient child — she kissed her mother on a hot, flushed cheek and left the house to go and find Harry.

Othelia's mother turned to reach for the stove and turned

off the fire that heated the cooking pot. She drew a breath painfully through tired lungs, staying conscious only long enough to see Tomari arrive through the door to the rest of the house, carrying another dinner that had been cooked for her family.

Othelia ran, her stomach churning and a feeling of upset rising into her chest. In her hand, she still held the pendant, its chain swinging as she ran. She ran so fast, that she did not even notice that she had crossed the boundary to the secret garden until she came to a standstill, with Harry perched forlornly a short distance before her, on a fallen, slanting tree-trunk.

He turned to look at her and his face mirrored the feelings that were swimming inside her. He held out a hand to her silently and as she walked towards him, she saw that he, too, was wearing a chain with a crystal pendant.

As she approached him, he took the chain that dangled from her fingers and motioned for her to turn round, so he could fasten it around her neck.

When she turned back round to look at him, his expression had lightened remarkably and he smiled at his little friend, prodding her cheek softly with his third finger to make her smile.

Smile, she did.

"I like her very much — the dancing girl," Harry said, swallowing a gulp in his throat, but smiling anyway. "Her bracelet was just like this one." He touched the coloured gems on Othelia's wrist, asking, "Do you want to see?"

Othelia, pleased now, looked at Harry with sparkling eyes and took in a breath of exhilaration at the thought of seeing the dancing girl.

"Yes, please, Harry," she said, nodding at him.

Harry rose to his feet and grabbed the little girl's hand.

"We must run, Othelia," he said, his chest ballooning, as though it would make him light enough to fly. "We must run to see the things that are worth seeing."

Othelia braced herself — and not a moment too soon, for then, each with a hand wrapped round their own crystal pendant, they were running, crossing the woodland at speed, as though their feet barely touched the ground.

Then, suddenly, although they were still moving, it was as though they had stopped and everything was swirling about them, until they were in the centre of a vortex, the shell of which was a swirling mass giving rise to silent pictures and scenes from a time long ago.

Othelia watched as she saw the shepherd paint his paintings in Elvador — his house abloom with tributes to his beloved land. She watched, as deer in the woods of Zohor danced excitedly as they sensed the presence of a young prince arriving to see them. She watched Queen Nelatron tend a garden of potent fragrance, its energies emanating to permeate Zohor with their flavoursome benevolence. She watched the old king hold court, receive his subjects with kindness in his eyes and enter the room of magical mystery, where he presented his son with a crystal pendant, once upon a time, long ago. The shades of the pictures changed then to a magenta hue, encasing a scene which played much slower than the ones previously. Three pochal trees stood in a small spot of woodland, guarded by a perimeter of closely-set bushes and trees. At the centre of where the three trees stood, Othelia saw a young man, dressed in green, crouching over the soil with a young woman who had a bow in her hair. There, between the trees, the pair planted a large, clear crystal the young man had produced from an inner fold of his jacket.

The young man then took the young lady's hand, the wrist of which was adorned by a bracelet of coloured gems and she led him out, through the bushes surrounding the Orchard of Pochals.

The vortex stopped swirling and disappeared, leaving Harry holding Othelia's braceleted hand in the secret garden.

"You must go," he turned to her and said, the beginnings of a pained expression showing in his eyes.

For the second time that day, Othelia was being asked to leave when she did not wish to. Ever obedient, however, she flung Harry a hug, exited the garden with his help and made her way back to the house. Her mind was saturated with flashing images of her mother's liquid eyes, Harry's torn ones, historic scenes from Zohor and characters from The Book of Stamps. Her slow footsteps were weighed down by the contemplation of a little girl's puzzled mind coupled with an emotion she could not put a word to. Only Harry was wise enough to describe things she did not understand.

Back in the secret garden, Harry's own mind clouded over. A storm brewed in the sky, darkening above. The little, burdened being in the flower cap tore the cap from his head, clasping his black hair tightly against his head in his hands. Still, the scenes from a long-past Zohor flashed in his mind: the prince, in the room of mystery, holding the bracelet of his love in one hand and a message from a place he loved in the other…

The prince, newly attuned to his telepathic powers, gingerly set up the table of crystals to link, first to Melthon. There, he, too, had shared a secret with the princess of Melthon. Together, they had buried a crystal from the palace in the Orchard of Pochals and the prince linked to it now, Maria's bracelet in his hand, to ask for a suitor for the woman who held his heart.

It came to him promptly — the vision, of a smiling man, dressed in green, a hint of mischief in his eyes.

The young prince threw his head back with a groan of relief, holding his breath for some time after to contain the mixture of ecstasy and happiness that swirled through him. Compose himself, he had to, for he still had a job to do. Summoning all the strength he could, he laid the bracelet down and picked up the envelope from Elvador, opening it with shaking fingers.

Although the vision he had just seen should have filled him with an all-consuming joy, he felt a crunch in his stomach as he extracted the letter from the envelope. Hesitating for a moment, he unfolded the parchment and read the message with growing alarm.

He did not even need to set up the crystal link to Elvador — he saw it all instantly. His companions, Palthon and Romonon and their fellow sons of courtiers, practising the slaying of animals on wooden targets in the hidden woods of the palace grounds. The energy of it, embedded in the crystal for Elvador as it sat in the hands of the prince himself the night before his journey there, transferred to the rich land of pastures, enabling the Hunters, his companions — Palthon and Romonon — to carry out their gruesome intentions.

The prince felt sick for the visions were coming rapidly now. He saw the advances Palthon and Romonon had made on the young women of Melthon, while Maria had introduced him to pochals. The rejection of the Hunters by the women had angered the companions of the prince and they had plotted their revenge.

The prince watched with horror, unable to understand how the kindly king's kingdom had given rise to such hideousness — and that, too, from within the palace grounds.

It was then the prince was shown images of other planets, on which beings who looked like the people of Zohor walked. One in particular was home to people who would kill, cheat and lie to serve their own needs. A mass of negativity from this planet shot in wavelengths through the cosmos into Zohor. The planet on which Zohor was located, with its tiny land-space and small number of people, did not stand a chance to remain unaffected by the dark vibration from the brother planet.

The prince watched, as visions of the near future flooded his mind. Uncontrollable, the sons of courtiers planned a rampage on Melthon, their spears now hunting an animal of their own kind. Infiltrated by evil from another planet, their minds had turned to hatred, anger and destruction. The energy had already detonated life in Elvador. The next port of call was Melthon.

"Who are you?" the prince demanded in desperation of the unseen forces which could project past and future to him so clearly. "If you knew of this, why would you let it happen? If you are all-wise, you cannot be all-good…"

The young prince broke down and wept before smacking the tears from his eyes with his hands, staring, determined, at the forces he could not see. Anger had taken hold of him, too.

"Show me," he said, "what I am to do. I demand that you rectify the injustice you have allowed."

"Your desire is what can heal it." A voice from an unseen source spoke in the boy's mind.

"My father's desire was not enough to save Elvador!" the

prince cried.

"Only through the wishes in your heart can you bring about your own visions," the voice replied.

The prince stopped for a moment as he felt, pounding in his heart, the deepest regret for the plight of Elvador. In his mind's eye, he saw four happy bears greeting him and fields and rocks roamed by carefree life. From the bottom of his soul, he felt his desire for it to be so.

There came then, for the first time in the history of the palace, a knocking at the door of the room of mystery.

The prince, roused by it, picked Maria's bracelet up, dropped it into his shirt and went to open the door.

One of his attendants stood quivering at the doorway, mayhem apparent in the corridor behind him.

"My Prince…" the attendant began.

The prince was hit by the deadly realisation that the images of the future he had just witnessed were already underway.

"I know." The kind prince assured his attendant, laying a hand on the younger boy's shoulder to minimise the feeling of terror he could see mirrored in the eyes that looked into his.

Sons of courtiers had formed a band of horses that had left for Melthon, already. They had kicked their horses' hooves high, armed themselves with spears and alarmed the rest of the palace folk with their obvious intention to wage war.

"Gather for me those who are of benevolence in this city to ride with me to Melthon," the prince instructed his attendant. "Inform my father," he added, "but tell him gently."

With those words, the prince left for Melthon, followed swiftly by other sons of the City of the Palace who wished to help him.

The king, for once oblivious to the activities around him, was still lost in the fragrances of the quiet herb garden, secluded at the back of the palace.

The young prince's attendant found the king and queen there and, still quivering, he relayed the information he needed to tell them.

The king and queen rose to their feet at once to attend to the situation.

"Thallon has left already?" the old queen asked in shock, aware of her family's duty, but concerned for her son.

"My Queen." The old king turned to her, his liquid eyes swimming with both alarm and emotion. "The prince is charmed: nothing can harm him."

He looked deep into his wife's eyes. They both knew that an era was about to end — that the shedding of their mantles had been symbolic in ending the peaceful, blessed reign of Orion.

Prince Thallon and his consorts thundered towards Melthon. They attempted the long journey unbroken, until weariness, hunger and thirst forced them to stop periodically to allow a short rest, the consumption of some fruit from trees, or a drink of refreshment from a spring. Even though he was limited by the needs of his body, the prince found no feeling of nourishment in the food gathered for him by the men he travelled with. Neither did he feel rested from the turmoil in his mind when his wearied body was forced to dismount his steed, now and again.

One of his fellow travellers — the young son of a courtier, delicate like his prince and a dear friend who was like a brother to him — spoke sense to the worried man in green, by reasoning, "Prince Thallon, what will you do when you arrive at Melthon if you have no strength?"

The thoughtful, young boy, Meritius, drew from his jacket a condensed slab made of nuts and sugar that his mother often cooked for him and offered it to the downcast prince.

The prince looked at Meritius, his younger friend, whose eyes fed an honesty into the prince's mind to displace some of the betrayal lodged there by Palthon, Romonon and their friends.

Wisdom would speak through any medium and the wisdom of Meritius' eyes enabled the prince to eat the slab of nuts, much to Meritius' relief. They drank from a nearby spring and were soon on their way again, but with the prince strengthened somewhat and a glimmer of light cutting through the darkness that had been shrouding his mind.

Eventually, the team of rescuers drew up to Melthon where, in place of merry people dancing, a black cloud darkened the approach to the village of berries.

An eerie silence guarded the perimeter of the village.

The prince and his friends entered Melthon on their horses quietly — the prince's brow furrowed, his heart beating like a tribal drum. He pressed a hand against his shirt where Maria's bracelet was still held close to his chest.

They made their way into the centre of Melthon and soon, they heard the commotion that had erupted there shortly before they saw it.

A carnage of injured villagers, speared through, staggered helplessly as the sons of courtiers — the Hunters — stampeded on horseback, dishevelling anything in sight. This day, it was not the juice of berries that flowed in the village, but another deep, red liquid, bleeding from the villagers of Melthon themselves.

The prince and his team of rescuers cried out loud at the sight they beheld — never could they have imagined or foreseen the manifestation of such evil or injustice. All but the prince had brought with them spears and other weapons, previously used for competitive games of innocence.

"My Prince!" Meritius called, throwing one of the two spears he had brought with him to the heir to the throne.

The young prince caught the spear, still in disbelief that the events before him were truly happening.

The prince and his fellow warriors charged then — at the men with whom the prince had schooled and lived alongside: brothers, torn by the two forces of creation — good and evil.

As his army began its fight, the prince, mid-charge, saw the wounded form of the alchemist beckon to him desperately. The prince pulled his horse round swiftly to face the man, who held his bleeding abdomen.

"Maria — she's in the orchard," the alchemist spluttered to the prince, "you must save her, Prince."

He looked at the prince pleadingly for a moment before Meritius cried to the prince to alert him to an oncoming charge from Palthon.

The young prince swung his horse round and for a brief moment his eyes met with the reddened ones of his former companion. There was no time to compose himself from the anger the Hunter sparked in him in this situation, so the prince blinked to block out the picture of the approaching Palthon and directed his horse towards the traitor to thunder an attack on the attacker. Head down, the prince focused his every intuition and mustered strength from such sources as Palthon could not even dream of. The young prince may not have excelled in records of spear-throwing as his opponent had, but his was a fight of good over evil and he charged with the faith of a cosmic justice, power surging through him, until, suddenly, time seemed to slow down. He raised his eyes again, saw Palthon's poise, swerved to avoid the traitor's spear, and delivered a puncture through the heart of the Hunter in one, determined plunge.

The red eyes of Palthon widened in surprise at the impact and the sound of meaty flesh encompassing metal — something he was growing used to — bade him goodbye in karmic return. The young prince's hand, which had never before harmed anything, had taken a life. The sport of the Hunter, so infectious, had infected the unwilling and forced upon the prince an inescapable destiny.

The battle continued. Almost all at Melthon had been wounded, the small village roused through, the villagers chased from their homes and slain by the hungry zeal of those who should have been their protectors. The Hunters fought with passion — a passion of anger: blood-thirsty, insatiable, uncontrollable…

The prince's army fought in the name of justice, called upon by the age-old laws that governed creation: inexplicable, incomprehensible, uncontrollable…

Before long, the Hunters, too, lay slain. They had been skilled, but weak of heart and possessed by a blinding rage. The prince's army, their wits intact and many in number with a determination coursing through them, had been more than a match for the army of his previous companions.

"Prince Thallon…" the broken voice of the alchemist rose from the moaning around him. "Maria… please save Maria."

"Maria is safe, dear alchemist," the young prince reassured the concerned father, dismounting his horse and walking unsteadily, with now trembling knees, towards where the bleeding man lay amongst the wounded.

"No, my Prince." The bloodshot eyes of the alchemist spoke of despair as he grasped the hand of the prince. About them, the prince's soldiers were dismounting their horses — some clutching scrapes and gashes, while others crouched to tend to the dying people of Melthon.

"Romonon…" The alchemist pointed with a last breath in the direction of the orchard.

As Maria's father wilted before him, the shock of what he had just heard propelled the young prince back onto his horse to charge towards the orchard.

His mind swirled with the horror of not just what he had witnessed in the centre of Melthon, but also with a hideous vision that was forming in his mind.

His head down, he bolted his horse at full speed, failing to notice along the way, that Romonon had not found the orchard, but was mid-search and watched the prince go by. The Hunter struck up pursuit at a distance and the prince remained unaware of the presence on his trail, even on arrival at the entrance to the orchard. He dismounted quickly, parting the hedgerow to step into the calm of the small land of pochals.

There, stood Maria, the dancing girl, the princess of Melthon, oblivious to the demise of her village. In her hands, she held up a suit of leaves she had been sewing; it had a green flower cap to match.

"Maria," the prince breathed, blood gushing to his cheeks as many emotions welled inside him, beckoning a weariness that made him feel as though he would collapse.

The dancing girl turned in surprise to see the man of her dreams, a shadow of the mischievous prince who had played his piccolo in the orchard before. His gentle face was smeared with dirt in which there were set scratches and he looked as though he had aged beyond his years.

The dancing girl gathered the leafy garments into a bundle in her arms and ran the short distance to her prince.

"My Prince... you're here," she said, concerned at the state of him. "What has befallen you, my dear, dear Prince?" she asked as she smoothed a lock of hair that was plastered with sweat on his forehead away from his face.

The prince looked for a moment, soul-tellingly into the divine young woman's eyes and felt unable to tell her of the horror that had come for her people. He had wanted to protect her from anything that could hurt her in life — not be the messenger of the worst tidings she could hear.

He mustered a strength that came from deeper than within his slender form. Folding her hand into his, he kissed it, pulled her bracelet out from inside his shirt, slipped it onto her wrist and said, "Nothing, my Princess. I wished to see you, that is all."

The princess of Melthon smiled, albeit unsurely, searching her prince's eyes for the truth.

The prince lowered his eyes to prevent her from reading them and focused on the package of curiosities she held.

"What are these?" he asked, for a moment detached from the events that had brought him there.

"They are for you, as you are a man of the wood. I thought it fitting to make you a suit from the things you love — so the trees can care for you wherever you are," Maria explained.

Tears sprung to the prince's eyes and he crumpled, like a withered flower before the dancing girl.

Unable to watch him hurt, she gathered him into her arms

to hold him close to her until it felt as though they had merged into one another, the warmth of her being filling his depleted spirit. She felt his pain filter into her heart and drawing a hand up to his face, she wiped his tears and cupped his cheek.

"Sweet Prince," she said gently, to the boy who was so sad, "one day, all things that ever went wrong... are put right."

For one illuminating moment, held in the strength of the woman who loved him, the young prince was lit from within by the wisdom of the ages, spoken through lips so sweet.

Suddenly, the bushes at the entrance to the orchard tore apart to reveal Romonon ready for his next kill.

The prince had dropped his spear seeing Maria safe before him and it now lay at the feet of Romonon, the man who should have been protector to the prince.

"Ah," rasped the Hunter, as the couple in the orchard pulled apart from their embrace to look at the invader in shock. "It seems that only a prince is good enough for the women of Melthon."

The hideous vision that had formed in the prince's mind on his way to the orchard was rapidly materialising before him.

"You will not touch her, Romonon," the prince spoke with a voice of steel to the Hunter, anger burning in his eyes.

"You are no longer my master. You no longer command me," the Hunter replied, his eyes reddened, too, hungry for power and charged with lust.

The young prince saw flashes before him of his childhood, his beautiful mother, the magical room of mystery... Instinctively, he pushed Maria behind him as Romonon lunged towards him. The Hunter tripped and his spear, which had already gathered momentum, was thrust forward, piercing the stomach of Zohor's young prince. Behind the prince was pressed Maria; the spear flowed through the prince, then through her heart.

The spirit of the young prince fell into the suit of leaves that was held between them.

Surrounded by spirits of the wood, the spirit of the prince, now clad in the leafy garments made so lovingly for him by the dancing girl, was lifted into the ether. He watched as the bodies of Maria and Thallon fell as one, encased in one another, in the middle of the space between three pochal trees, their blood staining the olive skin of the prince and nut-brown complexion of the dancing girl. He watched as Romonon thudded to the ground onto a sharpened rock which seared the Hunter to his death, too. The wood spirits carried their new companion over the trees, to Melthon's centre, where most of the residents of the village of berries lay lifeless. He watched, as time sped up in front of him and he saw that, not only had the Hunters been infected with destruction, but that a deathly energy had come for all of the City of the Palace. A virus, perfectly formed, generated from a surge of negativity from a planet far off, had spread to multiply in the blood of all from the City of the Palace, the prince's army included. Its incubation period complete, it erupted as an uncontrollable disease, killing the prince's parents, their courtiers and the people of the city.

The prince's army, themselves infected with the virus, passed the entity onto those few of Melthon who had survived the attack of the Hunters.

Within the space of one week, all the people of the City of the Palace and the villagers of Melthon had been obliterated, one way or another, with not one left to tell the tale.

The wood spirits supported their new charge for a while,

so that he might absorb knowledge of the events he saw before him. So tired afterwards was the spirit clad in the suit of leaves and flower cap, that the wood spirits carried him to a secluded garden surrounded at the perimeter by exquisite blossoms of the colours of the rainbow. There, the spirits laid their tired charge to rest in the hollow of an old tree, covering him in a blanket of flower-petals so that he might sleep for centuries, to awaken one day at a destined time, when his story could continue...

Harry took his head out of his hands. His face was plastered with tears.

A gentle wind blew softly onto his face to soothe his puffed cheeks. Two or three birds sat by him chirping furiously, as if to drown out his thoughts.

Two spirits of the wood had been stood in the trees, watching the distraught little being, his flower cap thrown to the ground. They had allowed him time for his emotions and now approached him to comfort him and draw him away from his pain — for a while, at least.

Little Harry allowed his friends, the spirits of the woods, to gather him up into their arms, place his flower cap back onto his glistening, black hair and take him to a place of comfort where his mind would be rested for a time.

Othelia's mother was no longer in the kitchen when her little daughter returned from her visit to see Harry. The melting pot lay abandoned, a wooden spoon beside it, on the stove. The pot was cold now.

"Mummy!" Othelia called, feeling lonely and more in need of her mother than ever.

A flustered and worried-looking Tomari came bundling

down the stairs. She grasped the little girl into her arms, holding her close against her bosom for some moments, before kneeling in front of the child to brief her on what was going on in the house.

A deathly silence was apparent from upstairs.

"Your dear mother has been taken with fever once more," the benevolent, concerned Tomari explained to Othelia. "The doctor is here and your father is here, too. They are both upstairs with your mother."

Tomari saw a dazed expression in Othelia's eyes and thought it better to lighten the situation, so as not to frighten the little girl. She picked Othelia up, smiled at her and asked her what she would most like to eat that she was seldom allowed to have.

Othelia had an immediate answer; there were plenty of things her mother did not let her eat often, but today, she had acquired a particular taste for her mother's cooking.

So Tomari heated some of what was in the pot, after tasting it to make sure it was cooked properly and still fresh enough for the little girl to eat. She then entertained her small charge until the dusky evening hailed bedtime for young children. By the time Tomari tucked Othelia into bed, the little child was sleepy and wrapped in her kind guardian's love, had recovered considerably from the harsh energies the day had brought.

Tomari returned to the bedroom where Othelia's poorly mother lay, flanked by Othelia's father and the doctor.

"Shall I bring Othelia to see her?" Tomari asked, a wretched feeling inside of her, telling her to fetch the little girl.

She was powerless to do so, however, without the permission of Othelia's father.

Othelia's father could not think straight in his desperation, much less hear what Tomari was asking him. Othelia was thus left uninformed of what was happening in the bedroom full of grown-ups.

"Please help her!" Othelia's father said to the doctor. "Please do something..." He slid an arm under his wife to draw her close to him, saying, "Darling..." He felt her body slacken away from him. "No..."

"My son, I'm so sorry," the doctor said helplessly.

Othelia's father held the lifeless body of Othelia's mother in his arms. Suffocated by grief, only silence spoke of his pain in being separated from her.

In the corridor outside, between the bedrooms, a ghostly form of the delicate lady could be seen gliding, softy towards her daughter's bedroom. She passed through the shut door and Othelia, half-asleep, turned to see the transparent figure of her mother standing by the door.

Too far into the dream-world to notice that anything was out of the normal, the little girl told her mother, sleepily, "It's okay, Mummy, I don't need a bedtime story tonight."

Her mother glided over to the bed and said, "I just wanted to kiss you goodnight, my sweet darling."

Othelia closed her eyes in anticipation and that night, it felt as though it was the breeze that kissed her.

She did not see her mother's form evaporate into the air that circulated around the room before flowing out through the open window, into the inky moonlight of Comera.

Othelia, remembering a look of despair that had tainted Harry's eyes just before she had left him, murmured as she fell asleep again, "Don't worry, Harry — one day, all things that ever went wrong... are put right."